PENGUIN BOOKS

Just So Stories

Rudyard Kipling was born in Bombay in 1865. His father, John Lockwood Kipling, was the author and illustrator of *Beast and Man in India*, and his mother, Alice, was the sister of Lady Burne-Jones. In 1871 Kipling was brought home from India and spent five unhappy years with a foster family in Southsea, an experience he later drew on in *The Light that Failed* (1891). The years he spent at the United Services College, a school for officers' children, are depicted in *Stalky and Co.* (1899) and the character of Beetle is something of a self-portrait. It was during his time at the college that he began writing poetry and *Schoolboy Lyrics* was published privately in 1881. In the following year he started work as a journalist in India, and while there produced a body of work, stories, sketches and poems – notably *Plain Tales from the Hills* (1888) – which made him an instant literary celebrity when he returned to England in 1889. *Barrack-Room Ballads* (1892) contains some of his most popular pieces, including 'Mandalay', 'Gunga Din' and 'Danny Deever'. In this collection Kipling experimented with form and dialect, notably the cockney accent of the soldier poems, but the influence of hymns, music-hall songs, ballads and public poetry can be found throughout his verse.

In 1892 he married an American, Caroline Balestier, and from 1892 to 1896 they lived in Vermont, where Kipling wrote *The Jungle Book*, published in 1894. In 1901 came *Kim* and in 1902 the *Just So Stories*. Tales of every kind – including historical and science fiction – continued to flow from his pen but *Kim* is generally thought to be his greatest long work, putting him high among the chroniclers of British expansion.

From 1902 Kipling made his home in Sussex, but he continued to travel widely and caught his first glimpse of warfare in South Africa, where he wrote some excellent reportage on the Boer War. However, many of the views he expressed were rejected by anti-imperialists who accused him of jingoism and love of violence. Though rich and successful, he never again enjoyed the literary esteem of his early years. With the onset of the Great War his work became a great deal more sombre. The stories he subsequently wrote, *A Diversity of Creatures* (1917), *Debits and Credits* (1926) and *Limits and Renewals* (1932), are now thought by many to contain some of his finest writing. The death of his only son in 1915 also contributed to a new inwardness of vision.

Kipling refused to accept the role of Poet Laureate and other civil honours, but he was the first English writer to be awarded the Nobel Prize, in 1907. He died in 1936 and his autobiographical fragment *Something of Myself* was published the following year.

Peter Levi, classical scholar, archaeologist and poet, was born in 1931. He translated *The Psalms* and Pausanias' *Guide to Greece* for Penguin Classics, as well as a collection of Yevtushenko (with R. Milner-Gulland) for the Penguin Modern Poets. He also edited *The Penguin Book of English Christian Verse*. He wrote more than sixty books, including *The Light Garden of the Angel King*, an account of his travels in Afghanistan; *A Bottle in the Shade*; *The Penguin History of Greek Literature* and biographies of Alfred Lord Tennyson, John Milton and Edward Lear. Peter Levi was Professor of Poetry at the University of Oxford from 1984 to 1989. He died on 1 February 2000.

Rudyard Kipling

JUST SO STORIES
FOR LITTLE CHILDREN

EDITED
WITH AN INTRODUCTION AND NOTES
BY PETER LEVI

Illustrated by the author

PENGUIN BOOKS

PENGUIN BOOKS

Published by the Penguin Group
Penguin Books Ltd, 27 Wrights Lane, London W8 5TZ, England
Penguin Putnam Inc., 375 Hudson Street, New York, New York 10014, USA
Penguin Books Australia Ltd, Ringwood, Victoria, Australia
Penguin Books Canada Ltd, 10 Alcorn Avenue, Toronto, Ontario, Canada M4V 3B2
Penguin Books (NZ) Ltd, Private Bag 102902, NSMC, Auckland, New Zealand

Penguin Books Ltd, Registered Offices: Harmondsworth, Middlesex, England

First published by Macmillan 1902
Published in Penguin Classics 1987
Reprinted in Penguin Books 1989
Reprinted in Penguin Classics 2000

2

Printed in England by Clays Ltd, St Ives plc
Set in Linotron 202 Ehrhardt

Contents

Introduction

It is an honour to introduce a book by Kipling, and he has told us that this one was his favourite. There is something rather unexplained about Kipling all the same, both as a man and as a writer; early in life he had been such a brilliant success, and his proper pride had been so hurt, that perhaps he was not very open to criticism. Literature is usually more co-operative than we imagine, but Kipling, in spite of his remarkable public and national stature, was one of those artists of intensely personal vision, separate, really, from the mainstream of culture, who have flourished more visibly since our community of belief and the old social structure fell apart. He was the national spokesman in the end for an ideal that was already in fragments. One should not be deceived into thinking of him as an establishment writer; he was as individual as the painter Francis Bacon, and he could be as terrifying.

The suspicion that his oddity concealed greatness has never entirely died out. On a simple level, this is because of the efficiency of his prose, the accuracy of his observation, his vivid likenesses, his ability to summon up a scene or a character or a mood. He was, admittedly, under a cloud with young lions and fashionable critics from the twenties to the sixties, but only because their housemasters and uncles had recommended him. Poets have always seen the point of his poetry, which I think of as a hidden but healthy influence even in the thirties and forties. He widened the range of English literature, and his tone was as hypnotic as Swinburne's had been or as Eliot's was to be. If his verse ever did go out of fashion, it was for technical reasons. The language, as he wrote it, was very heavily stressed, at a time when the inhabitants of Bloomsbury were already cooing and swooping like doves; and now we are all cooers rather than thumpers. But Kipling is thrilling, musically as well as in other ways. Brecht wanted to base a major work on Kipling, and their verse has something in common.

If I try to set out what it is I admire in him, then it is best to begin with an honest account of experience. The first poetry I remember liking as a child (apart from Shakespeare, whom I enjoyed for his fantasy and comedy and oceanic noises) was by Scott, but Kipling and Hardy followed swiftly. All these writers have a strong and dramatic narrative sense, and exhilarating rhythms. At nine or ten I think *Puck of Pook's Hill* was already one of my favourite books; we had perhaps done it at school or my mother read it to me. I liked it so much and for so long that I hardly dare re-read it now. Since that time I have read all the Kipling that I came across, and have frequently re-read the poetry in search of his elusive secret. When stuck bookless in London for the odd night as an adult, I have often bought an early second-hand edition of Kipling's prose to read in bed; they never cost more than fifty pence each.

I admire his courage as a writer, his lifelong refusal to give up, and his intrepidity in confronting his obviously deep personal sufferings. I like him for being an imaginative gardener in Sussex and a yachtsman in the Channel and for his gaiety on his bicycle and in his early motor car and for 'Fly forward O my heart/From the Foreland to the Start'. I like his criticism of England, which was ceaseless, though I have also been told that he wrote the radio speeches of George V. It is surely amazing in such an individualist that he should come close to being *the* national poet. Adrian Mitchell says in the Oxford Hysteria of English Poetry that Tennyson went on so long he got bored with himself and changed his name to Kipling at half time. I see his point and only half think it unfair. Tennyson did in fact express a rumble of elderly approval for the patriotic verses of the youthful Kipling.

But the following anecdote says more for Kipling. In a London club where he used to be a member, I once noticed his picture on the wall and wondered whether anyone in the club still remembered him. 'Oh yes,' said my neighbour. 'Kipling introduced me to this club. He used to visit our mess in India, on the North-West Frontier; he used to come quite often. He never said much, he just sat and listened. We used to get called

Introduction

out for what was called a cutting-out expedition, chasing around on horses in the dark. Kipling would still be there late at night when we came in, and hear all about it. I must have done it dozens of times as a young man and Kipling never came with us, but he wrote about it with the most brilliant accuracy as I could never have done. Just by listening.' The man who related this was a famous writer. Kipling's social conversation in London was said to be disappointing, but among the English writers of the last hundred years there have been few better listeners. His ear for the dialect of private soldiers was probably defective, but that is another matter. He was a natural and perhaps too lively parodist, even in the *Just So Stories*.

The borders of Afghanistan and Tibet were exciting to Kipling, because in his day they were receding frontiers. In his youth the imperial horizons were still advancing, and Kipling was a born explorer. One of the strangest and saddest things I know about him is that at school, a military academy of no great merit called Westward Ho!, he learnt Russian, obviously with an eye to taking part in the Great Game of Central Asian spying. The hero of his *Stalky & Co.*, who became a general in the First World War and later criticized Kipling with pompous severity for running down the dear old school, did, in fact, do minor intelligence work in Afghanistan, as an assistant to Aurel Stein. Marcus Aurelius Stein was a Hungarian Jew, intoxicated by the archaeological finds of the Hungarian Central Asia Expedition in his boyhood. In order to work there as an archaeologist, he became a British national and worked as a spy disguised as an archaeologist. He was the greatest of all explorers of Central Asia. But Kipling's eyesight was not good enough, and he was summoned back to India at seventeen to become a journalist. My own view is that his identification of schoolboy antics with the Great Game in *Stalky & Co.* was correct. Much that went on in the North-West Frontier area was both romantic and childish or boyish.

It is important to grasp the outline of his life, even though there is room here for only the briefest sketch. He lived from 1865 to 1936. In his twenty-third year he was famous, publishing seventy stories in eight books; the public yelled for more, but his great vogue ended with the Boer War. He was slightly dotty on several subjects at forty; seriously ill at fifty; and lived tragically on until his death at seventy. Thus we must concentrate on his earlier years. Tennyson, Swinburne, Hopkins, Arnold, Browning and Lewis Carroll must all have read him at the height of his fame. Had he been a less successful writer of documentary fiction and just struggled on as a poet, we would think of him as the contemporary of Yeats, which he exactly was. He was just thirteen years older than Edward Thomas, and for that reason, and because of his own rougher and readier education, less conscious of the real problems of literature at that time. His only full-scale novel, *The Light that Failed*, is a sharp and impressive book, but it does not, to my mind, suggest that he could have been a great novelist. He lacked Tolstoy's stamina, the intellectual stature of H. G. Wells, let alone of Henry James, and the fineness of Virginia Woolf, though one is free to prefer him to any of them for his small-scale but astounding powers, for his fascinating subject-matter, and because he was geniunely a poet. If he was often implicitly sentimental, he was no more so than Hemingway, who inclined to tight-lipped heroes for similar reasons.

Kipling was called Rudyard after a lake in Staffordshire where his parents first met. His father was working then as a designer in the potteries and belonged to the solidly Victorian Arts and Crafts movement, whose focus was the Victoria and Albert Museum. He later worked at the Lahore Museum and elsewhere in British India, and is said to have designed the Indian throne room at Osborne. Little Rudyard was sent home alone to be educated, at a younger age than usual because of his health. He was bullied and terrified, and I do not believe that he ever recovered. But he spent Christmas at Southsea with the Burne-Jones family, and for the rest of his life he remembered the ageing William Morris sitting on a rocking-horse, telling the children the most blood-curdling of Norse sagas in his own words. The *Just So Stories* are tales that Kipling told his own children; they have an epic formality that he learnt early in life.

His school was barbarous, but at least one can say that the headmaster encouraged him to read. He left in 1882, at the age

Introduction

of seventeen. At once Kipling began to write journalism and his thrilling stories of Indian life. He was always an immensely abundant and varied writer, but his early years gave him a head start. At twenty-three he was back in London and nationally famous. Naturally, he set off on extensive and, in the end, worldwide travels. He fell for a brilliant American author and publisher called Charles Wolcott Balestier, who also interested Henry James, and in 1892, at the age of twenty-seven, he married Balestier's sister. Throughout the nineties he published *Many Inventions*, both *Jungle Books*, *Captains Courageous*, *Barrack-Room Ballads*, *Seven Seas* and *A Fleet in Being*, an extraordinary and dashing work. For Jubilee Day 1897, long before it fitted the national mood, he wrote the poem 'Recessional'. It is supposed to have been rescued from his waste-paper basket, but he came to consider it his best poem. In 1901 he published *Kim*, and in 1902 the *Just So Stories*. That year he settled at Bateman's in Sussex, from which arose *Puck of Pook's Hill*, published in 1906.

It can be seen that his output in the first ten years of his marriage was strongly inclined to the boyish and to children's stories, and that even what he wrote for adults was for boyish or childish adults. Many of these books were still knocking about school libraries in the thirties and forties; they had not been edged out by his later writings. The only contemporary parallel to Kipling for liveliness and sheer inventiveness was Chesterton. There is an irrepressible quality about them both that can be found in other authors only to a lesser degree, and always in social outsiders. These writers were like a powerful, admirable force of nature that official, stuffed-shirt England was unable to restrain. Other literature of the period may be finer or more aesthetic, but in Chesterton and in Kipling it was alive.

A strain of sadness hits Kipling's fantasy in the *Just So Stories*. He spent 1898–9 in New York with the Balestiers and his three children. His younger daughter, Elsie, became Mrs Bambridge and outlived him; his son John died in the First World War; and Josephine, the eldest, died in 1899 in New York. It was to his children that these were first told. When he came to write them, he underlined the part his younger

11

Just So Stories

daughter had played in their conception. She must have been learning to read, and 'How the First Letter was Written' and 'How the Alphabet was Made' were specially for her.

> Her brows are bound with bracken-fronds,
>   And golden elf-locks fly above;
> Her eyes are bright as diamonds
>   And bluer than the sky above.
>
> In moccasins and deer-skin cloak,
>   Unfearing, free and fair she flits,
> And lights her little damp-wood smoke
>   To show her Daddy where she flits.
>
> For far—oh, very far behind,
>   So far she cannot call to him,
> Comes Tegumai alone to find
>   The daughter that was all to him.

Light verse? Certainly. Sentimental? Pardonably so. The rawness of the pain could not have been so sharply conveyed in any other way. I do not think Kipling felt that private grief was a proper subject for poetry; that is one reason why he is not quite a great poet, however much we like him. Those horrifying English boarding schools buttoned him up too tightly, and at nearly forty he was to be found brooding over the elf-locks of his dead baby. The same mood in the same years is on display at Osborne, in Queen Victoria's grotesque mementoes of her own children. But one does not like people the less for being so vulnerably mawkish, and the suddenness of the intrusion of personal feeling and the swiftness of its disappearance in Kipling's verse is what is moving. One may suspect that Kipling overvalued his *Just So Stories* because of the personal associations that enveloped them even before they were written down. Most of these stories are not really as brilliant as the two *Jungle Books*. For one thing, they are deliberately worldwide and prehistoric, which is no advantage. Kipling teases the children with foreign place-names and shipping lines as if they were labels on his luggage. Some of the places are invented, and they are all fantasized; the children's curiosity is being deliberately titillated. 'And they became the most beautiful islands of

12

Borneo, Celebes, Sumatra, Java, and the rest of the Malay Archipelago, and you can look them out on the map!'

In this book, as in most of those written within a decade of it, Kipling is didactic in several ways. The problem about this is that he is also a self-educated man, addicted to whims and fantasies. These stories are a kind of bad-taste parody of Darwin's theory of the evolution of species, and the truth about that subject is so overwhelmingly interesting as to make fantasies about it insipid. Yet Kipling could not have written without Darwin. Even his whimsical origin of the alphabet, which is correct in principle but sentimental in all its details, oddly reflects ideas that were afloat in the late nineteenth century. While Kipling was writing the *Just So Stories*, the Rosetta Stone had not long been deciphered; Arthur Evans was discovering the earliest syllabic scripts of the Greeks, Linear Scripts A and B. They use syllabic signs, not an alphabet, but the principle of the origins of signs is the same, and one can see Kipling's real interest in ancient scripts from his illustrations to his own book. As for the genuineness of his enthusiasm for prehistory, the moment when his unattractive, ancient landscape suddenly turns out to be the Surrey hills is thrilling, I think, and real.

Chesterton was to the same degree self-educated, and had much less experience of life. They set one another off in this way, as in others. Little or nothing that Chesterton wrote has dated as badly as Kipling's imperialism, though Kipling's views were at least functional in nourishing a sense of imperial *noblesse oblige* and of the supremacy of paternalist reasoning in the entire class of young men who really did govern the British Empire. But Kipling never professed anything as perverse as Chesterton's views on slavery and serfdom and Merry England, though Chesterton, even at his silliest, expresses a deep-rooted decency that he fosters in his readers to this day. Chesterton felt himself a liberal, Kipling proclaimed himself conservative, and yet it was Kipling whose views were objectively progressive in their day and Chesterton who still appeals to our tattered conservative instincts. They both wrote baddish poetry in extremely similar terms about a mystical England underlying the landscape. This theme first apperars in the *Just So Stories*.

Their quarrel was about the Boer War, and it was Kipling's view of the war that made him so hated by the literary intellectuals of the next generation, who were mostly liberal. In 1909 Rupert Brooke, in his school-leaving performance at the sixth-form debating society at Rugby, made a stinging attack on Kipling, with his Boer War imperialism very much in mind; though later in life he reproved Siegfried Sassoon for sneering at the older man, having been converted by Edward Marsh to the sound and technique of certain poems. Ezra Pound, to whom the Boer War meant nothing much, was brought up with 'the bustuous noises of Kipling'; Kipling was, I think, an unnoticed influence on Pound, who always respected the poems to some degree. Eliot was brought up on 'Danny Deever'. The great crisis of politics for Chesterton was the Marconi Case, which turned him and his circle against the parliamentary liberal party. As a conservative Kipling took an equally strong line against liberal corruption. Both writers had a streak of anti-Semitism, and they cannot have been displeased to find their enemy was called Rufus Isaacs. Kipling attacked him memorably and savagely in his poem 'Gehazi'.

Chesterton mounted *his* main attack on Kipling in the *Daily Mail* and reprinted it in *Heretics* in 1905. He began by admitting that 'the first and fairest thing to say about Rudyard Kipling is that he has borne a brilliant part in recovering the lost provinces of poetry'. He then scourges Kipling for 'militarism' and makes the searching criticism that 'he admires England because she is strong, not because she is English'. As Chesterton continues, he becomes grossly unfair. He says Kipling 'knows England as an intelligent Englishman knows Venice. He has been to England a great many times; he has stopped there for long visits. But he does not belong to it, or to any place . . .' But Kipling's travels were not only pardonable, they were surely admirable. The world really was thrilling to him. That sense is distilled in *Kim* and in the *Just So Stories*. As for his lack of English roots, the unkindness of Chesterton's jibe is out of place. It is suburban. There is more England in *Stalky & Co.*

BRITISH HEART FOUNDATION
202-204 HIGH STREET
PORTOBELLO
EDINBURGH
EH15 1EX
TEL NO: 0131 669 9375
BRANCH NO: P25

27 02 2010 SAT #1

B.FICTION	2.50
SUBTOTAL	2.50
B.FICTION	2.50
SUBTOTAL	5.00
TOTAL >>	5.00
CASH	10.00
CHANGE	5.00

ITEM   2
CASHIER 1   8238 11:36TM

THANK YOU FOR CALLING
CHARITY NUMBER 225971

Approved Charity Number 220971

REFUND POLICY

BHF will give a refund for goods returned in their original condition within 28 days of purchase, provided the original BHF price ticket is attached and the receipt is produced. The following items are excluded from these additional rights:

- CDs
- DVDs
- Videos
- Books

This policy does not affect your statutory rights, which are as follows:

****

Refunds will be given if goods do not comply with the Sale Of Goods (1979, as amended):

- If they are not of satisfactory quality. Please note that some goods on sale are second hand - please examine carefully as they may have minor faults.
- If they are not as described.
- If they are not fit for purpose.

Please retain your original **BHF** price ticket attached and receipt as proof of purchase.

Approved Charity Number 220971

REFUND POLICY

BHF will give a refund for goods returned in their original condition within 28 days of purchase, provided the original BHF price ticket is attached and the receipt is produced. The following items are excluded from these additional rights:

- CDs
- DVDs
- Videos
- Books

This policy does not affect your statutory rights, which are as follows:

****

Refunds will be given if goods do not comply with the Sale Of Goods (1979, as amended):

- If they are not of satisfactory quality. Please note that some goods on sale are second hand - please examine carefully as they may have minor faults.
- If they are not as described.
- If they are not fit for purpose.

Please retain your original **BHF** price ticket attached and receipt as proof of purchase.

Approved Charity Number 220971

REFUND POLICY

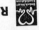

BHF will give a refund for goods returned in their original condition within 28 days of purchase, provided the original BHF price ticket is attached and the receipt is produced. The following items are excluded from these additional rights:

- CDs
- DVDs
- Videos
- Books

This policy does not affect your statutory rights, which are as follows:

****

Refunds will be given if goods do not comply with the Sale Of Goods (1979, as amended):

- If they are not of satisfactory quality. Please note that some goods on sale are second hand - please examine carefully as they may have minor faults.
- If they are not as described.
- If they are not fit for purpose.

than there is in *The Napoleon of Notting Hill*, which is a suburban fantasy after all. Even Chesterton's Christianity looks somehow provincial and limited today. His Europe was a small idea. One hopes that when *Puck of Pook's Hill* appeared in 1906, just a year after *Heretics*, Chesterton felt he had been answered.

Kipling uses the word 'nigger' in the *Just So Stories*, but so does Conrad in *The Nigger of the Narcissus*. Kipling intends no offence, and the word was normal in England in his day, but there is no doubt that Kipling had deeply offensive thoughts at the back of his head. He is unashamedly a colonialist, and part of our enjoyment is historical curiosity; he is a very interesting and articulate witness to a world and a set of values that had nearly withered away by the first decade of this century. When Leonard Woolf went out to Ceylon as a colonial officer in 1904, he took with him the voluminous works of Voltaire. He served for eight years, and his hand shook for the rest of his life from the shock of signing a death sentence. Cruelty lurks below the surface of several of the *Just So Stories*, and yet every story is somehow, somewhere, touched with authentic magic. I think this is partly a period quality that he communicates with clarity and immediacy. But it is also partly the magic of his style. He writes very well indeed, and that is why we still read him, and why our children will go on reading him until the language itself has altered too much.

Whether one likes to admit the fact or not, style is an aesthetic matter; there are no good natural stylists in English, and there have been none since the sixteenth century, perhaps none since Malory. The only exception I can think of is the prose style of John Clare, but even he learnt to read from newspapers and the exception may be more apparent than real. Kipling is as careful and conscious a stylist as Hemingway or Isaac Babel. His children's stories are not a million miles from Oscar Wilde's fables and several other such books that were popular in the nineties. His cluttered drawings belong, I suppose, to the style now called Art Deco. His pre-Raphaelite connections were probably as important to his prose style as they were to his drawing style. The formal conventions of the

Just So Stories appear to derive from the *Arabian Nights*, and bring to mind Flecker's *Hassan*. 'This, O Best Beloved, is another story of the High and Far-Off Times . . .' 'Once upon a most early time . . .' 'Hear and attend and listen; for this befell and behappened and became and was, O My Best Beloved, when the Tame animals were wild . . .' 'This, O my Best Beloved, is a story – a new and wonderful story – a story quite different from the other stories . . .' The formula is always varied, but it is always arresting, and often not only romantic but almost beautiful. To their first listeners they must have been intoxicating. It may be important that the children were not all the same age, because several stories have both very childish and rather grown-up elements in combination. There seems, for example, to be an ongoing joke about mispronunciation of long words that recalls *Brer Rabbit*. The stories were told in New York. The joke words occur mostly in the opening sentences of each tale, like 'stute', 'seruciating', 'sclusively', 'satiable', 'member' and 'curtiosity'. Kipling is not one to offer any other compromises over vocabulary; his children, like dons' children to this day, will have spoken like tiny adults. Kipling makes a bow towards baby-talk, but he has no interest in simplified language. Some of his jokes are crude and childish enough, but many are subtle. The same co-existence of adult and childish elements is to be found even in that smooth and masterly book, *The Wind in the Willows*.

It is harder than critics often think to analyse a style, and a narrative style perhaps hardest of all. In the line of descent from Stevenson to John Buchan, Kipling is a cousin of a kind. I assume in saying this that Stevenson is to be rated very highly, and that Buchan has some neglected virtues, though it may be a mere matter of generation that he does not sink to the insufferable and violent right-wing attitudes of such later writers as Sapper, Dornford Yates, and so on. Nor, of course, does Kipling, whose sense of justice is balanced, ironical and serene, more so in prose, perhaps, than in verse. English vernacular speech was rhythmic, lively and rather ungrammatical until it was organized and classicized through Latin examples and grammar school education from the late sixteenth century onwards. Kipling felt very strongly the supremacy of the Authorized Version of the Bible, which combines the new, solemn manner with many traces of the old sap and vigour. But the process of classicization continued to the time of Gibbon. The first signs of a vernacular revival in literature are to be found in slangy dandies like Byron, and in those realistic writings that led towards the novel.

At the same time classicism had become frigid and intolerably pompous. The great English novelists of the nineteenth century after Scott are not necessarily great stylists, and many of them have written pages of sentiment and stodge. Peacock is a later survival of classic English prose and there are others, but written and literary English was in a worse state in 1880 than in 1780. For example, one might consider a sermon in 1580, in 1680, in 1780 and in 1880, let alone in 1980. The best and the supplest narrative stylists in the nineteenth century were, I suppose, French, starting with Stendhal, and Russian, from Pushkin onwards; but Stevenson did a great deal for English, particularly in the unfinished *Weir of Hermiston*, which might have been the best novel in our language. The return to vernacular clarity and living rhythms in the narratives of Kipling and Stevenson was connected with their conception of a youthful audience. It was anti-school, unstuffy, and it liberated their remarkable imaginations. They desired to be swift and that is how they differ from lesser writers. At the bottom of all this lies an element, sometimes latent and sometimes dominant, in the work of Scott. By a freak of chance it was Scott who led me on to Kipling as a boy, and to Stevenson soon afterwards.

They are all romantic in more senses than one. The thrill of travel to remote islands, the glee of fantasy about animals and wild or strange peoples and mythologies, and the technical fascination of mechanical inventions can be traced backwards beyond the so-called Romantic movement, as far back as Rabelais and the Renaissance; but the opening up of the world that lay beyond the grand tour at the end of the nineteenth century gave a powerful stimulus to Kipling. India gave him a head start, and his youthful success gave him an opportunity that he seized. Even so, travel was not without its dangers. He was marooned by the failure of a bank in Yokohama, and had to creep home. There were places he never visited, and it was often on them that he concentrated his most potent nostalgia. 'And it's twenty thousand mile/To our little lazy isle/Where the Trumpet orchids blow.' Baudelaire had felt the same tug at his heart strings, and Gauguin and Stevenson died on their islands. Did Kipling have a hidden yearning to go back and settle? I think he really did, but he had taught himself to suppress it, and had chosen marriage to Balestier's sister. Sussex was his unsatisfactory substitute for paradise. I find it fascinating that Sir Richard Hannay's house in John Buchan's stories is like a cross between Buchan's own house and Kipling's house. Belloc's house was just as obviously romantic, but for Kipling romance was elsewhere.

> You'll know what my riddle means
> When you've eaten mangosteens.

Kipling watched the ships that left Southampton with the same nostalgic pangs as Baudelaire at Le Havre. For him, however, the voyage could easily have been possible, at least more so than for Baudelaire. To take ship was to cut away from life, to break oneself up, as Rimbaud and Gauguin had done.

> I've never sailed the Amazon,
> I've never reached Brazil;
> But the *Don* and *Magdalena*,
> They can go there when they will!
> Yes, weekly from Southampton,
> Great steamers, white and gold,
> Go rolling down to Rio
> (Roll down – roll down to Rio!)
> And I'd like to roll to Rio
> Some day before I'm old!

His classic statement of this sort of longing is not to be found here in this simple book, but wrapped up in the unforgettable words of 'Mandalay', and in

There's a whisper down the field where the year has shot her yield,
    And the ricks stand grey to the sun,

Singing: 'Over then, come over, for the bee has quit the clover,
    And your English summer's done.'

In the *Just So Stories* the theme is intertwined both in wildness and rawness and with domesticity and cosiness. This last is Kipling's feeling about home and children. I do not find this quite as convincing as the untamed elements in the same stories. He has not quite got it right, though he got it much more right in the writings that followed within a few years. In *Puck of Pook's Hill* the children are characters and that helps. In the *Just So Stories* only his dead daughter is a character, but painfully overstated. The Cave is not much like home. The best of all these stories is probably 'The Cat that Walked by Himself'. It is somehow typical of Kipling that he has an inwardness with cats, though he is agreeably fairminded about dogs. Those who possess both will recognize the fascination of their endless interplay. 'Ah!' said the Cat, listening. 'That is a very foolish Dog.' And he went back through the Wet Wild Woods waving his wild tail . . .' Kipling's woods are like the ones in *The Wind in the Willows*. Today, alas, they would be less wild, but they still exist; only his cat is everlasting and perfectly real. Of all animals we know, it has changed the least since prehistory. One cannot make friends with an armadillo or imagine the metamorphosis of an elephant or accept Kipling's version of Malayan mythology about the *Wonderful Tree at the Heart of the World*, but the cat, at least, is entirely believable. The drawings that illustrate the *Just So Stories* are playful and fantastical. They were probably made to amuse children watching the process of their being drawn. But the two for the Cat are extremely realistic. The second one, in which the Cat walks away down a long avenue of trees, might have been the illustration of a country essay by Alpha of the Plough, Kipling's forgotten contemporary.

It is a relief that Kipling was recognized, and not only in nurseries. He sensibly refused the Laureateship in 1895, and oddly the Order of Merit later, though he did accept that in the end. In 1907 Kipling received the Nobel Prize in his father's lifetime. What seems to have pleased him most was an honorary doctorate from the University of Paris in 1921, and an honorary fellowship of Magdalene College, Cambridge, in 1933, which throws some light on the later award of a similar fellowship to T. S. Eliot, and on Eliot's *Selected Poems of Kipling*, which he referred to as his war work. Kipling was not as great a writer, not as grand a social figure, and not as much a member of the establishment as he has seemed. He has always had something in common with the Cat that Walked by Himself, even though he often spoke for England in a way that no poet and no writer can do today. Sir John Betjeman did so, and so did George Orwell, but they were recognized almost too late. The only infallible test of literature is the test of time, the test of generations. Kipling has passed that test for just a hundred years.

In this edition I have added relatively few notes, because most of what at first sight seems to need explanation consists of jokes that a note would spoil or of teases that are meant to arouse but not to satisfy curiosity.

Peter Levi
February 1986

Note on the Text

The *Just So Stories For Little Children* was first published in volume form in 1902, containing twelve stories.
The original publication of the stories is as follows:
'How the Whale got his Throat': *St Nicholas* (a children's magazine), December 1897;
'How the Camel got his Hump': *St Nicholas*, January 1898;
'How the Rhinoceros got his Skin': *St Nicholas*, February 1898;
'How the Leopard got his Spots': *Pearson's Magazine*, April 1901;
'The Elephant's Child': *Ladies' Home Journal*, April 1900;
'The Sing-Song of Old Man Kangaroo': *Ladies' Home Journal*, June 1900;
'The Beginning of the Armadilloes': *Ladies' Home Journal*, May 1900;
'How the First Letter was Written': *Ladies' Home Journal*, December 1901;
'How the Alphabet was Made': *Just So Stories*, 1902;
'The Crab that Played with the Sea': *Pearson's Magazine*, August 1902 (where it was called 'The Crab that Played with the Tides');
'The Cat that Walked by Himself': *Ladies' Home Journal*, July 1902;
'The Butterfly that Stamped': *Ladies' Home Journal*, October 1902.
This edition of the *Just So Stories* follows the first edition of 1902.

JUST SO STORIES

How the Whale got his Throat

N the sea, once upon a time, O my Best Beloved, there was a Whale, and he ate fishes. He ate the starfish and the garfish, and the crab and the dab, and the plaice and the dace, and the skate and his mate, and the mackereel and the pickereel, and the really truly twirly-whirly eel. All the fishes he could find in all the sea he ate with his mouth – so! Till at last there was only one small fish left in all the sea, and he was a small 'Stute[1] Fish, and he swam a little behind the Whale's right ear, so as to be out of harm's way. Then the Whale stood up on his tail and said, 'I'm hungry.' And the small 'Stute Fish said in a small 'stute voice, 'Noble and generous Cetacean,[2] have you ever tasted Man?'

'No,' said the Whale. 'What is it like?'

'Nice,' said the small 'Stute Fish. 'Nice but nubbly.'

'Then fetch me some,' said the Whale, and he made the sea froth up with his tail.

'One at a time is enough,' said the 'Stute Fish. 'If you swim to latitude Fifty North, longitude Forty West (that is Magic), you will find, sitting *on* a raft, *in* the middle of the sea, with nothing on but a pair of blue canvas breeches, a pair of suspenders (you must *not* forget the suspenders, Best Beloved), and a jack-knife, one ship-wrecked Mariner, who, it is only fair to tell you, is a man of infinite-resource-and-sagacity.'

So the Whale swam and swam to latitude Fifty North, longitude Forty West,[7] as fast as he could swim, and *on* a raft, *in* the middle of the sea, *with* nothing to wear except a pair of blue

This is the picture of the Whale[3] swallowing the Mariner with his infinite-resource-and-sagacity, and the raft and the jack-knife *and* his suspenders,[4] which you must *not* forget. The buttony-things are the Mariner's suspenders, and you can see the knife close by them. He is sitting on the raft, but it has tilted up sideways, so you don't see much of it. The whity thing by the Mariner's left hand is a piece of wood that he was trying to row the raft with when the Whale came along. The piece of wood is called the jaws-of-a-gaff.[5] The Mariner left it outside when he went in. The Whale's name was Smiler, and the Mariner was called Mr Henry Albert Bivvens, A.B.[6] The little 'Stute Fish is hiding under the Whale's tummy, or else I would have drawn him. The reason that the sea looks so ooshy-skooshy is because the Whale is sucking it all into his mouth so as to suck in Mr Henry Albert Bivvens and the raft and the jack-knife and the suspenders. You must never forget the suspenders.

canvas breeches, a pair of suspenders (you must particularly remember the suspenders, Best Beloved), *and* a jack-knife, he found one single, solitary shipwrecked Mariner, trailing his toes in the water. (He had his Mummy's leave to paddle, or else he would never have done it, because he was a man of infinite-resource-and-sagacity.)

Then the Whale opened his mouth back and back and back till it nearly touched his tail, and he swallowed the shipwrecked Mariner, and the raft he was sitting on, and his blue canvas breeches, and the suspenders (which you *must* not forget), *and* the jack-knife. He swallowed them all down into his warm, dark inside cupboards, and then he smacked his lips – so, and turned round three times on his tail.

But as soon as the Mariner, who was a man of infinite-resource-and-sagacity, found himself truly inside the Whale's warm, dark, inside cupboards, he stumped and he jumped and he thumped and he bumped, and he pranced and he danced, and he banged and he clanged, and he hit and he bit, and he leaped and he creeped, and he prowled and he howled, and he hopped and he dropped, and he cried and he sighed, and he crawled and he bawled, and he stepped and he lepped, and he danced hornpipes where he shouldn't, and the Whale felt most unhappy indeed. (*Have* you forgotten the suspenders?)

So he said to the 'Stute Fish, 'This man is very nubbly, and besides he is making me hiccough. What shall I do?'

'Tell him to come out,' said the 'Stute Fish.

So the Whale called down his own throat to the shipwrecked Mariner, 'Come out and behave yourself. I've got the hic-coughs.'

'Nay, nay!' said the Mariner. 'Not so, but far otherwise. Take me to my natal-shore and the white-cliffs-of-Albion, and I'll think about it.' And he began to dance more than ever.

'You had better take him home,' said the 'Stute Fish to the Whale. 'I ought to have warned you that he is a man of infinite-resource-and-sagacity.'

So the Whale swam and swam and swam, with both flippers and his tail, as hard as he could for the hiccoughs; and at last he saw the Mariner's natal-shore and the white-cliffs-of-Albion, and he rushed half-way up the beach, and opened his mouth wide and wide and wide, and said, 'Change here for Winchester, Ashuelot, Nashua, Keene, and stations on the *Fitch*-burg Road'; and just as he said 'Fitch' the Mariner walked out of his mouth. But while the Whale had been swimming, the Mariner, who was indeed a person of infinite-resource-and-sagacity, had taken his jack-knife and cut up the raft into a little square grating all running criss-cross, and he had tied it firm with his suspenders (*now* you know why you were not to forget the suspenders!), and he dragged that grating good and tight into the Whale's throat, and there it stuck! Then he recited the following *Sloka*,[8] which, as you have not heard it, I will now proceed to relate:

> 'By means of a grating
> I have stopped your ating.'

For the Mariner he was also an Hi-ber-ni-an. And he stepped out on the shingle, and went home to his Mother, who had given him leave to trail his toes in the water; and he married and lived happily ever afterward. So did the Whale. But from that day on, the grating in his throat, which he could neither cough up nor swallow down, prevented him eating anything except very, very small fish; and that is the reason why whales now-adays never eat men or boys or little girls.

The small 'Stute Fish went and hid himself in the mud under the Door-sills of the Equator. He was afraid that the Whale might be angry with him.

The Sailor took the jack-knife home. He was wearing the blue canvas breeches when he walked out on the shingle. The suspenders were left behind, you see, to tie the grating with; and that is the end of *that* tale.

Here is the Whale looking for the little 'Stute Fish, who is hiding under the Door-sills of the Equator. The little 'Stute Fish's name was Pingle. He is hiding among the roots of the big seaweed that grows in front of the Doors of the Equator. I have drawn the Doors of the Equator. They are shut. They are always kept shut, because a door ought always to be kept shut. The ropy thing right across is the Equator itself; and the things that look like rocks are the two giants Moar and Koar, that keep the Equator in order. They drew the shadowpictures on the Doors of the Equator, and they carved all those twisty fishes under the Doors. The beaky fish are called beaked Dolphins, and the other fish with the queer heads are called Hammer-headed Sharks. The Whale never found the little 'Stute Fish till he got over his temper, and then they became good friends again.

When the cabin port-holes are dark and green
    Because of the seas outside;
When the ship goes *wop* (with a wiggle between)
And the steward falls into the soup-tureen,
    And the trunks begin to slide;
When Nursey lies on the floor in a heap,
And Mummy tells you to let her sleep,
And you aren't waked or washed or dressed,
Why, then you will know (if you haven't guessed)
You're 'Fifty North and Forty West!'

⟨ How the Camel got his Hump ⟩

OW this is the next tale, and it tells how the Camel got his big hump.

In the beginning of years, when the world was so new-and-all, and the Animals were just beginning to work for Man, there was a Camel, and he lived in the middle of a Howling Desert because he did not want to work; and besides, he was a Howler himself. So he ate sticks and thorns and tamarisks and milkweed and prickles, most 'scruciating idle; and when anybody spoke to him he said 'Humph!' Just 'Humph!' and no more.

Presently the Horse came to him on Monday morning, with a saddle on his back and a bit in his mouth, and said, 'Camel, O Camel, come out and trot like the rest of us.'

'Humph!' said the Camel; and the Horse went away and told the Man.

Presently the Dog came to him, with a stick in his mouth, and said, 'Camel, O Camel, come and fetch and carry like the rest of us.'

'Humph!' said the Camel; and the Dog went away and told the Man.

Presently the Ox came to him, with the yoke on his neck, and said, 'Camel, O Camel, come and plough like the rest of us.'

'Humph!' said the Camel; and the Ox went away and told the Man.

At the end of the day the Man called the Horse and the Dog

This is the picture of the Djinn making the beginnings of the Magic that brought the Humph to the Camel. First he drew a line in the air with his finger, and it became solid; and then he made a cloud, and then he made an egg – you can see them at the bottom of the picture – and then there was a magic pumpkin that turned into a big white flame. Then the Djinn took his magic fan and fanned that flame till the flame turned into a Magic by itself. It was a good Magic and a very kind Magic really, though it had to give the Camel a Humph because the Camel was lazy. The Djinn in charge of All Deserts was one of the nicest of the Djinns, so he would never do anything really unkind.

and the Ox together, and said, 'Three, O Three, I'm very sorry for you (with the world so new-and-all); but that Humph-thing in the Desert can't work, or he would have been here by now, so I am going to leave him alone, and you must work double-time to make up for it.'

That made the Three very angry (with the world so new-and-all), and they held a palaver, and an *indaba*, and a *punchayet*[1], and a pow-wow on the edge of the Desert; and the Camel came chewing milkweed *most* 'scruciating idle, and laughed at them. Then he said 'Humph!' and went away again.

Presently there came along the Djinn in charge of All Deserts, rolling in a cloud of dust (Djinns always travel that way because it is Magic), and he stopped to palaver and pow-wow with the Three.

'Djinn of All Deserts,' said the Horse, '*is* it right for any one to be idle, with the world so new-and-all?'

'Certainly not,' said the Djinn.

'Well,' said the Horse, 'there's a thing in the middle of your Howling Desert (and he's a Howler himself) with a long neck and long legs, and he hasn't done a stroke of work since Monday morning. He won't trot.'

'Whew!' said the Djinn, whistling, 'that's my Camel, for all the gold in Arabia! What does he say about it?'

'He says "Humph!"' said the Dog; 'and he won't fetch and carry.'

'Does he say anything else?'

'Only "Humph!"; and he won't plough,' said the Ox.

'Very good,' said the Djinn. 'I'll humph him if you will kindly wait a minute.'

The Djinn rolled himself up in his dustcloak, and took a bearing across the desert, and found the Camel most 'scruciatingly idle, looking at his own reflection in a pool of water.

'My long and bubbling friend,' said the Djinn, 'what's this I hear of your doing no work, with the world so new-and-all?'

'Humph!' said the Camel.

The Djinn sat down, with his chin in his hand, and began to think a Great Magic, while the Camel looked at his own reflection in the pool of water.

'You've given the Three extra work ever since Monday morning, all on account of your 'scruciating idleness,' said the Djinn; and he went on thinking Magics, with his chin in his hand.

'Humph!' said the Camel.

'I shouldn't say that again if I were you,' said the Djinn; 'you might say it once too often. Bubbles, I want you to work.'

And the Camel said 'Humph!' again; but no sooner had he said it than he saw his back, that he was so proud of, puffing up and puffing up into a great big lolloping humph.

'Do you see that?' said the Djinn. 'That's your very own humph that you've brought upon your very own self by not working. Today is Thursday, and you've done no work since Monday, when the work began. Now you are going to work.'

'How can I,' said the Camel, 'with this humph on my back?'

'That's made a-purpose,' said the Djinn, 'all because you missed those three days. You will be able to work now for three days without eating, because you can live on your humph; and don't you ever say I never did anything for you. Come out of the Desert and go to the Three, and behave. Humph yourself!'

And the Camel humphed himself, humph and all, and went away to join the Three. And from that day to this the Camel always wears a humph (we call it 'hump' now, not to hurt his feelings); but he has never yet caught up with the three days that he missed at the beginning of the world, and he has never yet learned how to behave.

Here is the picture of the Djinn in charge of All Deserts guiding the Magic with his magic fan. The Camel is eating a twig of acacia, and he has just finished saying 'Humph!' once too often (the Djinn told him he would), and so the Humph is coming. The long towelly-thing growing out of the thing like an onion is the Magic, and you can see the Humph on its shoulder. The Humph fits on the flat part of the Camel's back. The Camel is too busy looking at his own beautiful self in the pool of water to know what is going to happen to him.

Underneath the truly picture is a picture of the World-so-new-and-all. There are two smoky volcanoes in it, some other mountains and some stones and a lake and a black island and a twisty river and a lot of other things, as well as a Noah's Ark. I couldn't draw all the deserts that the Djinn was in charge of, so I only drew one, but it is a most deserty desert.

The Camel's hump is an ugly lump
   Which well you may see at the Zoo;
But uglier yet is the hump we get
   From having too little to do.

Kiddies and grown-ups too-oo-oo,
If we haven't enough to do-oo-oo,
      We get the hump—
      Cameelious hump—
The hump that is black and blue!

We climb out of bed with a frouzly head
   And a snarly-yarly voice.
We shiver and scowl and we grunt and we growl
   At our bath and our boots and our toys;

And there ought to be a corner for me
(And I know there is one for you)
      When we get the hump—
      Cameelious hump—
The hump that is black and blue!

The cure for this ill is not to sit still,
   Or frowst with a book by the fire;
But to take a large hoe and a shovel also,
   And dig till you gently perspire;

And then you will find that the sun and the wind,
And the Djinn of the Garden too,
      Have lifted the hump—
      The horrible hump—
The hump that is black and blue!

I get it as well as you-oo-oo—
If I haven't enough to do-oo-oo!
      We all get hump—
      Cameelious hump—
Kiddies and grown-ups too!

❴ How the Rhinoceros got his Skin ❵

NCE upon a time, on an uninhabited island on the shores of the Red Sea, there lived a Parsee[1] from whose hat the rays of the sun were reflected in more-than-oriental splendour. And the Parsee lived by the Red Sea with nothing but his hat and his knife and a cooking-stove of the kind that you must particularly never touch. And one day he took flour and water and currants and plums and sugar and things, and made himself one cake which was two feet across and three feet thick. It was indeed a Superior Comestible (*that*'s Magic), and he put it on the stove because *he* was allowed to cook on that stove, and he baked it and he baked it till it was all done brown and smelt most sentimental. But just as he was going to eat it there came down to the beach from the Altogether Uninhabited Interior one Rhinoceros with a horn on his nose, two piggy eyes, and few manners. In those days the Rhinoceros's skin fitted him quite tight. There were no wrinkles in it anywhere. He looked exactly like a Noah's Ark Rhinoceros, but of course much bigger. All the same, he had no manners then, and he has no manners now, and he never will have any manners. He said, 'How!' and the Parsee left that cake and climbed to the top of a palm-tree with nothing on but his hat, from which the rays of the sun were always reflected in more-than-oriental splendour. And the Rhinoceros upset the oil-stove with his nose, and the cake rolled on the sand, and he spiked that cake on the horn of his nose, and he ate it, and he went away, waving his tail, to the desolate and Exclusive Uninhabited Interior which abuts on the islands of Mazanderan, Socotra, and the Promontories of the Larger Equinox.[2] Then the Parsee came down from his palm-tree and put the stove on its legs and recited the following *Sloka*, which, as you have not heard, I will now proceed to relate:

> 'Them that takes cakes
> Which the Parsee-man bakes
> Makes dreadful mistakes.'

And there was a great deal more in that than you would think.

Because, five weeks later, there was a heatwave in the Red Sea, and everybody took off all the clothes they had. The Parsee took off his hat; but the Rhinoceros took off his skin and carried it over his shoulder as he came down to the beach to bathe. In those days it buttoned underneath with three buttons and looked like a waterproof. He said nothing whatever about the Parsee's cake, because he had eaten it all; and he never had any manners, then, since, or henceforward. He waddled straight into the water and blew bubbles through his nose, leaving his skin on the beach.

Presently the Parsee came by and found the skin, and he smiled one smile that ran all round his face two times. Then he danced three times round the skin and rubbed his hands. Then he went to his camp and filled his hat with cake-crumbs, for the Parsee never ate anything but cake, and never swept out his camp. He took that skin, and he shook that skin, and he scrubbed that skin, and he rubbed that skin just as full of old, dry, stale, tickly cake-crumbs and some burned currants as ever it could *possibly* hold. Then he climbed to the top of his palm-tree and waited for the Rhinoceros to come out of the water and put it on.

And the Rhinoceros did. He buttoned it up with the three buttons, and it tickled like cake-crumbs in bed. Then he wanted to scratch, but that made it worse; and then he lay down on the sands and rolled and rolled and rolled, and every time he rolled the cake-crumbs tickled him worse and worse and worse. Then he ran to the palm-tree and rubbed and rubbed and rubbed himself against it. He rubbed so much and so hard that he rubbed his skin into a great fold over his shoulders, and another fold underneath, where the buttons used to be (but he rubbed the buttons off), and he rubbed some more folds over his legs. And it spoiled his temper, but it didn't make the least difference to the cake-crumbs. They were inside his skin and they tickled. So he went home, very angry indeed and horribly scratchy; and from that day to this every rhinoceros has great folds in his skin and a very bad temper, all on account of the cake-crumbs inside.

But the Parsee came down from his palm-tree, wearing his hat, from which the rays of the sun were reflected in more-than-oriental splendour, packed up his cooking-stove, and went away in the direction of Orotavo, Amygdala, the Upland Meadows of Anantarivo, and the Marshes of Sonaput.[3]

This is the picture of the Parsee beginning to eat his cake on the Uninhabited Island in the Red Sea on a very hot day; and of the Rhinoceros coming down from the Altogether Uninhabited Interior, which, as you can truthfully see, is all rocky. The Rhinoceros's skin is quite smooth, and the three buttons that button it up are underneath, so you can't see them. The squiggly things on the Parsee's hat are the rays of the sun reflected in more-than-oriental splendour, because if I had drawn real rays they would have filled up all the picture. The cake has currants in it; and the wheel-thing lying on the sand in front belonged to one of Pharaoh's chariots when he tried to cross the Red Sea. The Parsee found it, and kept it to play with. The Parsee's name was Pestonjee Bomonjee, and the Rhinoceros was called Strorks, because he breathed through his mouth instead of his nose. I wouldn't ask anything about the cooking-stove if *I* were you.

This is the Parsee Pestonjee Bomonjee sitting in his palm-tree and watching the Rhinoceros Strorks bathing near the beach of the Altogether Uninhabited Island after Strorks had taken off his skin. The Parsee has rubbed the cake-crumbs into the skin, and he is smiling to think how they will tickle Strorks when Strorks puts it on again. The skin is just under the rocks below the palm-tree in a cool place; that is why you can't see it. The Parsee is wearing a new more-than-oriental-splendour hat of the sort that Parsees wear; and he has a knife in his hand to cut his name on palm-trees. The black things on the islands out at sea are bits of ships that got wrecked going down the Red Sea; but all the passengers were saved and went home.

The black thing in the water close to the shore is not a wreck at all. It is Strorks the Rhinoceros bathing without his skin. He was just as black underneath his skin as he was outside. I wouldn't ask anything about the cooking-stove if *I* were you.

This Uninhabited Island
    Is off Cape Gardafui,
By the Beaches of Socotra
    And the Pink Arabian Sea:[4]
But it's hot – too hot from Suez
    For the likes of you and me
        Ever to go
        In a P. & O.
    And call on the Cake-Parsee.

⸬ How the Leopard got his Spots ⸬

N the days when everybody started fair, Best Beloved, the Leopard lived in a place called the High Veldt.[1] 'Member it wasn't the Low Veldt, or the Bush Veldt, or the Sour Veldt, but the 'sclusively bare, hot, shiny High Veldt, where there was sand and sandy-coloured rock and 'sclusively tufts of sandy-yellowish grass. The Giraffe and the Zebra and the Eland and the Koodoo and the Hartebeest[2] lived there; and they were 'sclusively sandy-yellow-brownish all over; but the Leopard, he was the 'sclusivest sandiest-yellowest-brownest of them all – a greyish-yellowish catty-shaped kind of beast, and he matched the 'sclusively yellowish-greyish-brownish colour of the High Veldt to one hair. This was very bad for the Giraffe and the Zebra and the rest of them; for he would lie down by a 'sclusively yellowish-greyish-brownish stone or clump of grass, and when the Giraffe or the Zebra or the Eland or the Koodoo or the Bush-Buck or the Bonte-Buck[3] came by he would surprise them out of their jumpsome lives. He would indeed! And, also, there was an Ethiopian with bows and arrows (a 'sclusively greyish-brownish-yellowish man he was then), who lived on the High Veldt with the Leopard; and the two used to hunt together – the Ethiopian with his bows and arrows, and the Leopard 'sclusively with his teeth and claws – till the Giraffe and the Eland and the Koodoo and the Quagga[4] and all the rest of them didn't know which way to jump, Best Beloved. They didn't indeed!

After a long time – things lived for ever so long in those days – they learned to avoid anything that looked like a Leopard or

an Ethiopian; and bit by bit – the Giraffe began it, because his
legs were the longest – they went away from the High Veldt.
They scuttled for days and days and days till they came to a
great forest, 'sclusively full of trees and bushes and stripy,
speckly, patchy-blatchy shadows, and there they hid: and after
another long time, what with standing half in the shade and half
out of it, and what with the slippery-slidy shadows of the trees
falling on them, the Giraffe grew blotchy, and the Zebra grew
stripy, and the Eland and the Koodoo grew darker, with little
wavy grey lines on their backs like bark on a tree trunk; and so,
though you could hear them and smell them, you could very
seldom see them, and then only when you knew precisely
where to look. They had a beautiful time in the 'sclusively
speckly-spickly shadows of the forest, while the Leopard and
the Ethiopian ran about over the 'sclusively greyish-yellowish-
reddish High Veldt outside, wondering where all their break-
fasts and their dinners and their teas had gone. At last they
were so hungry that they ate rats and beetles and rock-rabbits,
the Leopard and the Ethiopian, and then they had the Big
Tummy-ache, both together; and then they met Baviaan – the
dog-headed, barking Baboon, who is Quite the Wisest Animal
in All South Africa.

Said Leopard to Baviaan (and it was a very hot day), 'Where
has all the game gone?'

And Baviaan winked. *He* knew.

Said the Ethiopian to Baviaan, 'Can you tell me the present
habitat of the aboriginal Fauna?' (That meant just the same
thing, but the Ethiopian always used long words. He was a
grown-up.)

And Baviaan winked. *He* knew.

Then said Baviaan, 'The game has gone into other spots;
and my advice to you, Leopard, is to go into other spots as soon
as you can.'

And the Ethiopian said, 'That is all very fine, but I wish to
know whither the aboriginal Fauna has migrated.'

Then said Baviaan, 'The aboriginal Fauna has joined the
aboriginal Flora because it was high time for a change; and my
advice to you, Ethiopian, is to change as soon as you can.'

That puzzled the Leopard and the Ethiopian, but they set off to look for the aboriginal Flora, and presently, after ever so many days, they saw a great, high, tall forest full of tree trunks all 'sclusively speckled and sprottled and spottled, dotted and splashed and slashed and hatched and cross-hatched with shadows. (Say that quickly aloud, and you will see how *very* shadowy the forest must have been.)

'What is this,' said the Leopard, 'that is so 'sclusively dark, and yet so full of little pieces of light?'

'I don't know,' said the Ethiopian, 'but it ought to be the aboriginal Flora. I can smell Giraffe, and I can hear Giraffe, but I can't see Giraffe.'

'That's curious,' said the Leopard. 'I suppose it is because we have just come in out of the sunshine. I can smell Zebra, and I can hear Zebra, but I can't see Zebra.'

'Wait a bit,' said the Ethiopian. 'It's a long time since we've hunted 'em. Perhaps we've forgotten what they were like.'

'Fiddle!' said the Leopard. 'I remember them perfectly on the High Veldt, especially their marrow-bones. Giraffe is about seventeen feet high, of a 'sclusively fulvous[5] golden-yellow from head to heel; and Zebra is about four and a half feet high, of a 'sclusively grey-fawn colour from head to heel.'

'Umm,' said the Ethiopian, looking into the speckly-spickly shadows of the aboriginal Flora-forest. 'Then they ought to show up in this dark place like ripe bananas in a smoke-house.'

But they didn't. The Leopard and the Ethiopian hunted all day; and though they could smell them and hear them, they never saw one of them.'

'For goodness' sake,' said the Leopard at tea-time, 'let us wait till it gets dark. This daylight hunting is a perfect scandal.'

So they waited till dark, and then the Leopard heard something breathing sniffily in the starlight that fell all stripy through the branches, and he jumped at the noise, and it smelt like Zebra, and it felt like Zebra, and when he knocked it down it kicked like Zebra, but he couldn't see it. So he said, 'Be quiet, O you person without any form. I am going to sit on your head till morning, because there is something about you that I don't understand.'

This is Wise Baviaan, the dog-headed Baboon, who is Quite the Wisest Animal in All South Africa. I have drawn him from a statue that I made up out of my own head, and I have written his name on his belt and on his shoulder and on the thing he is sitting on. I have written it in what is not called Coptic and Hieroglyphic and Cunieformic and Bengalic and Burmic and Hebric,[6] all because he is so wise. He is not beautiful, but he is very wise; and I should like to paint him with paint-box colours, but I am not allowed. The umbrella-ish thing about his head is his Conventional Mane.

Presently he heard a grunt and a crash and a scramble, and the Ethiopian called out, 'I've caught a thing that I can't see. It smells like Giraffe, and it kicks like Giraffe, but it hasn't any form.'

'Don't you trust it,' said the Leopard. 'Sit on its head till the morning – same as me. They haven't any form – any of 'em.'

So they sat down on them hard till bright morning-time, and then Leopard said, 'What have you at your end of the table, Brother?'

The Ethiopian scratched his head and said, 'It ought to be 'sclusively a rich fulvous orange-tawny from head to heel, and it ought to be Giraffe; but it is covered all over with chestnut blotches. What have you at *your* end of the table, Brother?'

And the Leopard scratched his head and said, 'It ought to be 'sclusively a delicate greyish-fawn, and it ought to be Zebra; but it is covered all over with black and purple stripes. What in the world have you been doing to yourself Zebra? Don't you know that if you were in the High Veldt I could see you ten miles off? You haven't any form.'

'Yes,' said the Zebra, 'but this isn't the High Veldt. Can't you see?'

'I can now,' said the Leopard. 'But I couldn't all yesterday. How is it done?'

'Let us up,' said the Zebra, 'and we will show you.'

They let the Zebra and the Giraffe get up; and Zebra moved away to some little thornbushes where the sunlight fell all stripy, and Giraffe moved off to some tallish trees where the shadows fell all blotchy.

'Now watch,' said the Zebra and the Giraffe. 'This is the way it's done. One – two – three! And where's your breakfast?'

Leopard stared, and Ethiopian stared, but all they could see were stripy shadows and blotched shadows in the forest, but never a sign of Zebra and Giraffe. They had just walked off and hidden themselves in the shadowy forest.

'Hi! Hi!' said the Ethiopian. 'That's a trick worth learning. Take a lesson by it, Leopard. You show up in this dark place like a bar of soap in a coal-scuttle.'

'Ho! Ho!' said the Leopard. 'Would it surprise you very

54

much to know that you show up in this dark place like a mustard-plaster on a sack of coals?'

'Well, calling names won't catch dinner,' said the Ethiopian. 'The long and the little of it is that we don't match our backgrounds. I'm going to take Baviaan's advice. He told me I ought to change; and as I've nothing to change except my skin I'm going to change that.'

'What to?' said the Leopard, tremendously excited.

'To a nice working blackish-brownish colour, with a little purple in it, and touches of slaty-blue. It will be the very thing for hiding in hollows and behind trees.'

So he changed his skin then and there, and the Leopard was more excited than ever; he had never seen a man change his skin before.

'But what about me?' he said, when the Ethiopian had worked his last little finger into his fine new black skin.

'You take Baviaan's advice too. He told you to go into spots.'

'So I did,' said the Leopard. 'I went into other spots as fast as I could. I went into this spot with you, and a lot of good it has done me.'

'Oh,' said the Ethiopian, 'Baviaan didn't mean spots in South Africa. He meant spots on your skin.'

'What's the use of that?' said the Leopard.

'Think of Giraffe,' said the Ethiopian. 'Or if you prefer stripes, think of Zebra. They find their spots and stripes give them per-fect satisfaction.'

'Umm,' said the Leopard. 'I wouldn't look like Zebra – not for ever so.'

'Well, make up your mind,' said the Ethiopian, 'because I'd hate to go hunting without you, but I must if you insist on looking like a sunflower against a tarred fence.'

'I'll take spots, then,' said the Leopard; 'but don't make 'em too vulgar-big. I wouldn't look like Giraffe – not for ever so.'

'I'll make 'em with the tips of my fingers,' said the Ethiopian. 'There's plenty of black left on my skin still. Stand over!'

Then the Ethiopian put his five fingers close together (there was plenty of black left on his new skin still) and pressed them all over the Leopard, and wherever the five fingers touched

This is the picture of the Leopard and the Ethiopian after they had taken Wise Baviaan's advice and the Leopard had gone into other spots and the Ethiopian had changed his skin. The Ethiopian was really a negro, and so his name was Sambo. The Leopard was called Spots, and he has been called Spots ever since. They are out hunting in the spickly-speckly forest, and they are looking for Mr One-Two-Three-Where's-your-Breakfast. If you look a little you will see Mr One-Two-Three not far away. The Ethiopian has hidden behind a splotchy-blotchy tree because it matches his skin, and the Leopard is lying beside a spickly-speckly bank of stones because it matches his spots. Mr One-Two-Three-Where's-your-Breakfast is standing up eating leaves from a tall tree. This is really a puzzle-picture like 'Find-the-Cat.'

they left five little black marks, all close together. You can see them on any Leopard's skin you like, Best Beloved. Sometimes the fingers slipped and the marks got a little blurred; but if you look closely at any Leopard now you will see that there are always five spots – off five fat black finger-tips.

'Now you *are* a beauty!' said the Ethiopian. 'You can lie out on the bare ground and look like a heap of pebbles. You can lie out on the naked rocks and look like a piece of pudding-stone.[7] You can lie out on a leafy branch and look like sunshine sifting through the leaves; and you can lie right across the centre of a path and look like nothing in particular. Think of that and purr!'

'But if I'm all this,' said the Leopard, 'why didn't you go spotty too?'

'Oh, plain black's best for a nigger,' said the Ethiopian. 'Now come along and we'll see if we can't get even with Mr One-Two-Three-Where's-your-Breakfast!'

So they went away and lived happily ever afterward, Best Beloved. That is all.

Oh, now and then you will hear grown-ups say, 'Can the Ethiopian change his skin or the Leopard his spots?'[8] I don't think even grown-ups would keep on saying such a silly thing if the Leopard and the Ethiopian hadn't done it once – do you? But they will never do it again, Best Beloved. They are quite contented as they are.

I am the Most Wise Baviaan, saying in most wise tones,
'Let us melt into the landscape – just us two by our lones.'
People have come – in a carriage – calling. But Mummy is
    there . . .
Yes, I can go if you take me – Nurse says *she* don't care.
Let's go up to the pig-sties and sit on the farmyard rails!
Let's say things to the bunnies, and watch 'em skitter their
    tails!
Let's – oh, *anything*, daddy, so long as it's you and me,
And going truly exploring, and not being in till tea!
Here's your boots (I've brought 'em), and here's your cap
    and stick,
And here's your pipe and tobacco. Oh, come along out of it –
    quick!

⁅ The Elephant's Child ⁆

N the High and Far-Off Times the Elephant, O Best Beloved, had no trunk. He had only a blackish, bulgy nose, as big as a boot, that he could wriggle about from side to side; but he couldn't pick up things with it. But there was one Elephant – a new Elephant – an Elephant's Child – who was full of 'satiable curtiosity, and that means he asked ever so many questions. *And* he lived in Africa, and he filled all Africa with his 'satiable curtiosities. He asked his tall aunt, the Ostrich, why her tail-feathers grew just so, and his tall aunt the Ostrich spanked him with her hard, hard claw. He asked his tall uncle, the Giraffe, what made his skin spotty, and his tall uncle, the Giraffe, spanked him with his hard, hard hoof. And still he was full of 'satiable curtiosity! He asked his broad aunt, the Hippopotamus, why her eyes were red, and his broad aunt, the Hippopotamus, spanked him with her, broad, broad hoof; and he asked his hairy uncle, the Baboon, why melons tasted just so, and his hairy uncle, the Baboon, spanked him with his hairy, hairy paw. And *still* he was full of 'satiable curtiosity! He asked questions about everything that he saw, or heard, or felt, or smelt, or touched, and all his uncles and his aunts spanked him. And still he was full of 'satiable curtiosity!

One fine morning in the middle of the Precession[1] of the Equinoxes this 'satiable Elephant's Child asked a new fine question that he had never asked before. He asked, 'What does the Crocodile have for dinner?' Then everybody said, 'Hush!'

in a loud and dretful tone, and they spanked him immediately and directly, without stopping, for a long time.

By and by, when that was finished, he came upon Kolokolo Bird sitting in the middle of a wait-a-bit thorn-bush,[2] and he said, 'My father has spanked me, and my mother has spanked me; all my aunts and uncles have spanked me for my 'satiable curtiosity; and *still* I want to know what the Crocodile has for dinner!'

Then Kolokolo Bird said, with a mournful cry, 'Go to the banks of the great grey-green, greasy Limpopo River, all set about with fever-trees, and find out.'

That very next morning, when there was nothing left of the Equinoxes, because the Precession had preceded according to precedent, this 'satiable Elephant's Child took a hundred pounds of bananas (the little short red kind), and a hundred pounds of sugar-cane (the long purple kind), and seventeen melons (the greeny-crackly kind), and said to all his dear families, 'Good-bye. I am going to the great grey-green, greasy Limpopo River,[3] all set about with fever-trees, to find out what the Crocodile has for dinner.' And they all spanked him once more for luck, though he asked them most politely to stop.

Then he went away, a little warm, but not at all astonished, eating melons, and throwing the rind about, because he could not pick it up.

He went from Graham's Town to Kimberley, and from Kimberley to Khama's Country,[4] and from Khama's Country he went east by north, eating melons all the time, till at last he came to the banks of the great grey-green, greasy Limpopo River, all set about with fever-trees, precisely as Kolokolo Bird had said.

Now you must know and understand, O Best Beloved, that till that very week, and day, and hour, and minute, this 'satiable Elephant's Child had never seen a Crocodile, and did not know what one was like. It was all his 'satiable curtiosity.

The first thing that he found was a Bi-Coloured-Python-Rock-Snake curled round a rock.

''Scuse me,' said the Elephant's Child most politely, 'but

have you seen such a thing as a Crocodile in these promiscuous parts?'

'*Have* I seen a Crocodile?' said the Bi-Coloured-Python-Rock-Snake, in a voice of dretful scorn. 'What will you ask me next?'

''Scuse me,' said the Elephant's Child, 'but could you kindly tell me what he has for dinner?'

Then the Bi-Coloured-Python-Rock-Snake uncoiled himself very quickly from the rock, and spanked the Elephant's Child with his scalesome, flailsome tail.

'That is odd,' said the Elephant's Child, 'because my father and mother, and my uncle and my aunt, not to mention my other aunt, the Hippopotamus, and my other uncle, the Baboon, have all spanked me for my 'satiable curtiosity – and I suppose this is the same thing.'

So he said goodbye very politely to the Bi-Coloured-Python-Rock-Snake, and helped to coil him up on the rock again, and went on, a little warm, but not at all astonished, eating melons, and throwing the rind about, because he could not pick it up, till he trod on what he thought was a log of wood at the very edge of the great grey-green, greasy Limpopo River, all set about with fever-trees.

But it was really the Crocodile, O Best Beloved, and the Crocodile winked one eye – like this!

''Scuse me,' said the Elephant's Child most politely, 'but do you happen to have seen a Crocodile in these promiscuous parts?'

Then the Crocodile winked the other eye, and lifted half his tail out of the mud; and the Elephant's Child stepped back most politely, because he did not wish to be spanked again.

'Come hither, Little One,' said the Crocodile. 'Why do you ask such things?'

''Scuse me,' said the Elephant's Child most politely, 'but my father spanked me, my mother has spanked me, not to mention my tall aunt, the Ostrich, and my tall uncle, the Giraffe, who can kick ever so hard, as well as my broad aunt, the Hippopotamus, and my hairy uncle, the Baboon, *and* including the

Bi-Coloured-Python-Rock-Snake, with the scalesome, flail-some tail, just up the bank, who spanks harder than any of them; and *so*, if it's quite all the same to you, I don't want to be spanked any more.'

'Come hither, Little One,' said the Crocodile, 'for I am the Crocodile,' and he wept crocodile-tears to show it was quite true.

Then the Elephant's Child grew all breathless, and panted, and kneeled down on the bank and said, 'You are the very person I have been looking for all these long days. Will you please tell me what you have for dinner?'

'Come hither, Little One,' said the Crocodile, 'and I'll whisper.'

Then the Elephant's Child put his head down close to the Crocodile's musky, tusky mouth, and the Crocodile caught him by his little nose, which up to that very week, day, hour, and minute, had been no bigger than a boot, though much more useful.

'I think,' said the Crocodile – and he said it between his teeth, like this – 'I think today I will begin with Elephant's Child!'

At this, O Best Beloved, the Elephant's Child was much annoyed, and he said, speaking through his nose, like this, 'Led go! You are hurtig be!'

Then the Bi-Coloured-Python-Rock-Snake scuffled down from the bank and said, 'My young friend, if you do not now, immediately and instantly, pull as hard as ever you can, it is my opinion that your acquaintance in the large-pattern leather ulster' (and by this he meant the Crocodile) 'will jerk you into yonder limpid stream before you can say Jack Robinson.'

This is the way Bi-Coloured-Python-Rock-Snakes always talk.

Then the Elephant's Child sat back on his little haunches, and pulled, and pulled, and pulled, and his nose began to stretch. And the Crocodile floundered into the water, making it all creamy with great sweeps of his tail, and *he* pulled, and pulled, and pulled.

And the Elephant's Child's nose kept on stretching; and the

This is the Elephant's Child having his nose pulled by the Crocodile. He is much surprised and astonished and hurt, and he is talking through his nose and saying, 'Led go! You are hurtig be!' He is pulling very hard, and so is the Crocodile; but the Bi-Coloured-Python-Rock-Snake is hurrying through the water to help the Elephant's Child. All that black stuff is the banks of the great grey-green, greasy Limpopo River (but I am not allowed to paint these pictures), and the bottly-tree with the twisty roots and the eight leaves is one of the fever trees that grow there.

Underneath the truly picture are shadows of African animals walking into an African ark. There are two lions, two ostriches, two oxen, two camels, two sheep, and two other things that look like rats, but I think they are rock-rabbits. They don't mean anything. I put them in because I thought they looked pretty. They would look very fine if I were allowed to paint them.

Elephant's Child spread all his little four legs and pulled, and pulled, and pulled, and his nose kept on stretching; and the Crocodile threshed his tail like an oar, and *he* pulled, and pulled, and pulled, and at each pull the Elephant's Child's nose grew longer and longer – and it hurt him hijjus!

Then the Elephant's Child felt his legs slipping, and he said through his nose, which was now nearly five feet long, 'This is too butch for be!'

Then the Bi-Coloured-Python-Rock-Snake came down from the bank, and knotted himself in a double-clove-hitch[5] round the Elephant's Child's hind-legs, and said, 'Rash and inexperienced traveller, we will now seriously devote ourselves to a little high tension, because if we do not, it is my opinion that yonder self-propelling man-of-war with the armour-plated upper deck' (and by this, O Best Beloved, he meant the Crocodile) 'will permanently vitiate your future career.'

That is the way all Bi-Coloured-Python-Rock-Snakes always talk.

So he pulled, and the Elephant's Child pulled, and the Crocodile pulled; but the Elephant's Child and the Bi-Coloured-Python-Rock-Snake pulled hardest; and at last the Crocodile let go of the Elephant's Child's nose with a plop that you could hear all up and down the Limpopo.

Then the Elephant's Child sat down most hard and sudden; but first he was careful to say 'Thank you' to the Bi-Coloured-Python-Rock-Snake; and next he was kind to his poor pulled nose, and wrapped it all up in cool banana leaves, and hung it in the great grey-green, greasy Limpopo to cool.

'What are you doing that for?' said the Bi-Coloured-Python-Rock-Snake.

''Scuse me,' said the Elephant's Child, 'but my nose is badly out of shape, and I am waiting for it to shrink.'

'Then you will have to wait a long time,' said the Bi-Coloured-Python-Rock-Snake. 'Some people do not know what is good for them.'

The Elephant's Child sat there for three days waiting for his nose to shrink. But it never grew any shorter, and, besides, it made him squint. For, O Best Beloved, you will see and understand that the Crocodile had pulled it out into a really truly trunk same as all Elephants have today.

At the end of the third day a fly came and stung him on the shoulder, and before he knew what he was doing he lifted up his trunk and hit that fly dead with the end of it.

''Vantage number one!' said the Bi-Coloured-Python-Rock-Snake. 'You couldn't have done that with a mere-smear nose. Try and eat a little now.'

Before he thought what he was doing the Elephant's Child put out his trunk and plucked a large bundle of grass, dusted it clean against his fore-legs, and stuffed it into his own mouth.

''Vantage number two!' said the Bi-Coloured-Python-Rock-Snake. 'You couldn't have done that with a mere-smear nose. Don't you think the sun is very hot here?'

'It is,' said the Elephant's Child, and before he thought what he was doing he schlooped up a schloop of mud from the banks of the great grey-green Limpopo, and slapped it on his head, where it made a cool schloopy-sloshy mud-cap all trickly behind his ears.

''Vantage number three!' said the Bi-Coloured-Python-Rock-Snake. 'You couldn't have done that with a mere-smear nose. Now how do you feel about being spanked again?'

''Scuse me,' said the Elephant's Child, 'but I should not like it at all.'

'How would you like to spank somebody?' said the Bi-Coloured-Python-Rock-Snake.

'I should like it very much indeed,' said the Elephant's Child.

'Well,' said the Bi-Coloured-Python-Rock-Snake, 'you will find that new nose of yours very useful to spank people with.'

'Thank you,' said the Elephant's Child, 'I'll remember that; and now I think I'll go home to all my dear families and try.'

So the Elephant's Child went home across Africa frisking and whisking his trunk. When he wanted fruit to eat he pulled fruit down from a tree, instead of waiting for it to fall as he used to do. When he wanted grass he plucked grass up from the ground, instead of going on his knees as he used to do. When the flies bit him he broke off the branch of a tree and used it as a

This is just a picture of the Elephant's Child going to pull bananas off a banana-tree after he had got his fine new long trunk. I don't think it is a very nice picture; but I couldn't make it any better, because elephants and bananas are hard to draw. The streaky things behind the Elephant's Child mean squoggy marshy country somewhere in Africa. The Elephant's Child made most of his mud-cakes out of the mud that he found there. I think it would look better if you painted the banana-tree green and the Elephant's Child red.

fly-whisk; and he made himself a new, cool, slushy-squshy mud-cap whenever the sun was hot. When he felt lonely walking through Africa he sang to himself down his trunk, and the noise was louder than several brass bands. He went specially out of his way to find a broad Hippopotamus (she was no relation of his), and he spanked her very hard, to make sure that the Bi-Coloured-Python-Rock-Snake had spoken the truth about his new trunk. The rest of the time he picked up the melon rinds that he had dropped on his way to the Limpopo – for he was a Tidy Pachyderm.[6]

One dark evening he came back to all his dear families, and he coiled up his trunk and said, 'How do you do?' They were very glad to see him, and immediately said, 'Come here and be spanked for your 'satiable curtiosity.'

'Pooh,' said the Elephant's Child. 'I don't think you peoples know anything about spanking; but *I* do, and I'll show you.'

Then he uncurled his trunk and knocked two of his dear brothers head over heels.

'O Bananas!' said they, 'where did you learn that trick, and what have you done to your nose?'

'I got a new one from the Crocodile on the banks of the great grey-green, greasy Limpopo River,' said the Elephant's Child. 'I asked him what he had for dinner, and he gave me this to keep.'

'It looks very ugly,' said his hairy uncle, the Baboon.

'It does,' said the Elephant's Child. 'But it's very useful,' and he picked up his hairy uncle, the Baboon, by one hairy leg, and hove him into a hornets' nest.'

Then that bad Elephant's Child spanked all his dear families for a long time, till they were very warm and greatly astonished. He pulled out his tall Ostrich aunt's tail-feathers; and he caught his tall uncle, the Giraffe, by the hind-leg, and dragged him through a thorn-bush; and he shouted at his broad aunt, the Hippopotamus, and blew bubbles into her ear when she was sleeping in the water after meals; but he never let anyone touch Kolokolo Bird.

At last things grew so exciting that his dear families went off one by one in a hurry to the banks of the great grey-green, greasy Limpopo River, all set about with fever-trees, to borrow new noses from the Crocodile. When they came back nobody spanked anybody any more; and ever since that day, O Best Beloved, all the Elephants you will ever see, besides all those that you won't, have trunks precisely like the trunk of the 'satiable Elephant's Child.

I keep six honest serving-men
  (They taught me all I knew);
Their names are What and Why and When
  And How and Where and Who.
I send them over land and sea,
  I send them east and west;
But after they have worked for me,
  I give them all a rest.

I let them rest from nine till five,
  For I am busy then,
As well as breakfast, lunch, and tea,
  For they are hungry men:
But different folk have different views;
  I know a person small –
She keeps ten million serving-men,
  Who get no rest at all!
She sends 'em abroad on her own affairs,
  From the second she opens her eyes –
One million Hows, two million Wheres,
  And seven million Whys!

The Sing-Song of Old Man Kangaroo

OT always was the Kangaroo as now we do behold him, but a different Animal with four short legs. He was grey and he was woolly, and his pride was inordinate: he danced on an outcrop in the middle of Australia, and he went to the Little God Nqa.

He went to Nqa at six before breakfast, saying, 'Make me different from all other animals by five this afternoon.'

Up jumped Nqa from his seat on the sand-flat and shouted, 'Go away!'

He was grey and he was woolly, and his pride was inordinate: he danced on a rock-ledge in the middle of Australia, and he went to the Middle God Nquing.

He went to Nquing at eight after breakfast, saying, 'Make me different from all other animals; make me, also, wonderfully popular by five this afternoon.'

Up jumped Nquing from his burrow in the spinifex and shouted, 'Go away!'

He was grey and he was woolly, and his pride was inordinate: he danced on a sandbank in the middle of Australia, and he went to the Big God Nqong.

He went to Nqong at ten before dinner-time, saying, 'Make me different from all other animals; make me popular and wonderfully run after by five this afternoon.'

Up jumped Nqong from his bath in the salt-pan and shouted, 'Yes, I will!'

Nqong called Dingo – Yellow-Dog Dingo[1] – always hungry,

73

This is a picture of Old Man Kangaroo when he was the Different Animal with four short legs. I had drawn him grey and woolly, and you can see that he is very proud because he has a wreath of flowers in his hair. He is dancing on an outcrop (that means a ledge of rock) in the middle of Australia at six o'clock before breakfast. You can see that it is six o'clock, because the sun is just getting up. The thing with the ears and the open mouth is Little God Nqa. Nqa is very much surprised, Nqa is just saying, 'Go away,' but the Kangaroo is so busy dancing that he has not heard him yet.

The Kangaroo hasn't any real name except Boomer.[2] He lost it because he was so proud.

dusty in the sunshine, and showed him Kangaroo. Nqong said, 'Dingo! Wake up, Dingo! Do you see that gentleman dancing on an ashpit? He wants to be popular and very truly run after. Dingo, make him so!'

Up jumped Dingo – Yellow-Dog Dingo – and said, 'What, *that* cat-rabbit?'

Off ran Dingo – Yellow-Dog Dingo – always hungry, grinning like a coal-scuttle, – ran after Kangaroo.

Off went the proud Kangaroo on his four little legs like a bunny.

This, O Beloved of mine, ends the first part of the tale!

He ran through the desert; he ran through the mountains; he ran through the salt-pans; he ran through the reed-beds; he ran through the blue gums; he ran through the spinifex;[3] he ran till his front legs ached.

He had to!

Still ran Dingo – Yellow-Dog Dingo – always hungry, grinning like a rat-trap, never getting nearer, never getting farther, – ran after Kangaroo.

He had to!

Still ran Kangaroo – Old Man Kangaroo. He ran through the ti-trees;[4] he ran through the mulga;[5] he ran through the long grass; he ran through the short grass; he ran through the Tropics of Capricorn and Cancer; he ran till his hind legs ached.

He had to!

Still ran Dingo – Yellow-Dog Dingo – hungrier and hungrier, grinning like a horse-collar, never getting nearer, never getting farther; and they came to the Wollgong River.[6]

Now, there wasn't any bridge, and there wasn't any ferry-boat, and Kangaroo didn't know how to get over; so he stood on his legs and hopped.

He had to!

He hopped through the Flinders;[7] he hopped through the Cinders; he hopped through the deserts in the middle of Australia. He hopped like a Kangaroo.

First he hopped one yard; then he hopped three yards; then he hopped five yards; his legs growing stronger; his legs growing longer. He hadn't any time for rest or refreshment, and he wanted them very much.

Still ran Dingo – Yellow-Dog Dingo – very much bewildered, very much hungry, and wondering what in the world or out of it made Old Man Kangaroo hop.

For he hopped like a cricket; like a pea in a saucepan; or a new rubber ball on a nursery floor.

He had to!

He tucked up his front legs; he hopped on his hind legs; he stuck out his tail for a balance-weight behind him; and he hopped through the Darling Downs.[8]

He had to!

Still ran Dingo – Tired-Dog Dingo – hungrier and hungrier, very much bewildered, and wondering when in the world or out of it would Old Man Kangaroo stop.

Then came Nqong from his bath in the salt-pans, and said, 'It's five o'clock.'

Down sat Dingo – Poor-Dog Dingo – always hungry, dusty in the sunshine; hung out his tongue and howled.

Down sat Kangaroo – Old Man Kangaroo – stuck out his tail like a milking-stool behind him, and said, 'Thank goodness *that*'s finished!'

Then said Nqong, who is always a gentleman, 'Why aren't you grateful to Yellow-Dog Dingo? Why don't you thank him for all he has done for you?'

Then said Kangaroo – Tired Old Kangaroo – 'He's chased me out of the homes of my childhood; he's chased me out of my regular meal-times; he's altered my shape so I'll never get it back; and he's played Old Scratch[9] with my legs.'

Then said Nqong, 'Perhaps I'm mistaken, but didn't you ask me to make you different from all other animals, as well as to make you very truly sought after? And now it is five o'clock.'

'Yes,' said Kangaroo. 'I wish that I hadn't. I thought you would do it by charms and incantations, but this is a practical joke.'

'Joke!' said Nqong, from his bath in the blue gums. 'Say that again and I'll whistle up Dingo and run your hind legs off.'

'No,' said the Kangaroo. 'I must apologise. Legs are legs,

This is the picture of Old Man Kangaroo at five in the afternoon, when he had got his beautiful hind legs just as Big God Nqong had promised. You can see that it is five o'clock, because Big God Nqong's pet tame clock says so. That is Nqong, in his bath, sticking his feet out. Old Man Kangaroo is being rude to Yellow-Dog Dingo. Yellow-Dog Dingo has been trying to catch Kangaroo all across Australia. You can see the marks of Kangaroo's big new feet running ever so far back over the bare hills. Yellow-Dog Dingo is drawn black, because I am not allowed to paint these pictures with real colours out of a paint-box; and besides, Yellow-Dog Dingo got dreadfully black and dusty after running through the Flinders and the Cinders.

I don't know the names of the flowers growing round Nqong's bath. The two little squatty things out in the desert are the other two gods that Old Man Kangaroo spoke to early in the morning. That thing with the letters on it is Old Man Kangaroo's pouch. He had to have a pouch just as he had to have legs.

and you needn't alter 'em so far as I am concerned. I only meant to explain to Your Lordliness that I've had nothing to eat since morning, and I'm very empty indeed.'

'Yes,' said Dingo – Yellow-Dog Dingo, – 'I am just in the same situation. I've made him different from all other animals; but what may I have for my tea?'

Then said Nqong from his bath in the salt-pan, 'Come and ask me about it tomorrow, because I'm going to wash.'

So they were left in the middle of Australia, Old Man Kangaroo and Yellow-Dog Dingo, and each said, 'That's *your* fault.'

This is the mouth-filling song
Of the race that was run by a Boomer,
Run in a single burst – only event of its kind –
Started by Big God Nqong from Warrigaborrigarooma,
Old Man Kangaroo first: Yellow-Dog Dingo behind.

Kangaroo bounded away,
His back-legs working like pistons–
Bounded from morning till dark,
Twenty-five feet to a bound.
Yellow-Dog Dingo lay
Like a yellow cloud in the distance –
Much too busy to bark.
My! but they covered the ground!

Nobody knows where they went,
Or followed the track that they flew in,
For that Continent
Hadn't been give a name.
They ran thirty degrees,
From Torres Straits to the Leeuwin
(Look at the Atlas, please),
And they ran back as they came.

S'posing you could trot
From Adelaide to the Pacific,
For an afternoon's run –
Half what these gentlemen did –
You would feel rather hot,
But your legs would develop terrific –
Yes, my importunate son,
You'd be a Marvellous Kid!

The Beginning of the Armadilloes

HIS, O Best Beloved, is another story of the High and Far-Off Times. In the very middle of those times was a Stickly-Prickly Hedgehog, and he lived on the banks of the turbid Amazon, eating shelly snails and things. And he had a friend, a Slow-Solid Tortoise, who lived on the banks of the turbid Amazon, eating green lettuce and things. And so *that* was all right, Best Beloved. Do you see?

But also, and at the same time, in those High and Far-Off Times, there was a Painted Jaguar, and he lived on the banks of the turbid Amazon too; and he ate everything that he could catch. When he could not catch deer or monkeys he would eat frogs and beetles; and when he could not catch frogs and beetles he went to his Mother Jaguar, and she told him how to eat hedgehogs and tortoises.

She said to him ever so many times, graciously waving her tail, 'My son, when you find a Hedgehog you must drop him into the water and then he will uncoil, and when you catch a Tortoise you must scoop him out of his shell with your paw.' And so that was all right, Best Beloved.

One beautiful night on the banks of the turbid Amazon, Painted Jaguar found Stickly-Prickly Hedgehog and Slow-and-Solid Tortoise sitting under the trunk of a fallen tree. They could not run away, and so Stickly-Prickly curled himself up into a ball, because he was a Hedgehog, and Slow-and-Solid Tortoise drew in his head and feet into his shell as far as

82

they would go, because he was a Tortoise; and so *that* was all right, Best Beloved. Do you see?

'Now attend to me,' said Painted Jaguar, 'because this is very important. My mother said that when I meet a Hedgehog I am to drop him into the water and then he will uncoil, and when I meet a Tortoise I am to scoop him out of his shell with my paw. Now which of you is Hedgehog and which is Tortoise? Because, to save my spots, I can't tell.'

'Are you sure of what your Mummy told you?' said Stickly-Prickly Hedgehog. 'Are you quite sure? Perhaps she said that when you uncoil a Tortoise you must shell him out of the water with a scoop, and when you paw a Hedgehog you must drop him on the shell.'

'Are you sure of what your Mummy told you?' said Slow-and-Solid Tortoise. 'Are you quite sure? Perhaps she said that when you water a Hedgehog you must drop him into your paw, and when you meet a Tortoise you must shell him till he uncoils.'

'I don't think it was at all like that,' said Painted Jaguar, but he felt a little puzzled; 'but, please, say it again more distinctly.'

'When you scoop water with your paw you uncoil it with a Hedgehog,' said Stickly-Prickly. 'Remember that, because it's important.'

'*But*,' said the Tortoise, 'when you paw your meat you drop it into a Tortoise with a scoop. Why can't you understand?'

'You are making my spots ache,' said Painted Jaguar; 'and besides, I didn't want your advice at all. I only wanted to know which of you is Hedgehog and which is Tortoise.'

'I shan't tell you,' said Stickly-Prickly. 'But you can scoop me out of my shell if you like.'

'Aha!' said Painted Jaguar. 'Now I know you're Tortoise. You thought I wouldn't! Now I will.' Painted Jaguar darted out his paddy-paw just as Stickly-Prickly curled himself up, and of course Jaguar's paddy-paw was just filled with prickles. Worse than that, he knocked Stickly-Prickly away and away into the woods and the bushes, where it was too dark to find him. Then he put his paddy-paw into his mouth, and of course the prickles hurt him worse than ever. As soon as he could speak he said,

This is an inciting map of the Turbid Amazon done in Red and Black. It hasn't anything to do with the story except that there are two Armadilloes in it – up by the top. The inciting part are the adventures that happened to the men who went along the road marked in red. I meant to draw Armadilloes when I began the map, and I meant to draw manatees and spider-tailed monkeys and big snakes and lots of Jaguars, but it was more inciting to do the map and the venturesome adventures in red. You begin at the bottom left-hand corner and follow the little arrows all about, and then you come quite round again to where the adventuresome people went home in a ship called the *Royal Tiger*. This is a most adventuresome picture, and all the adventures are told about in writing, so you can be quite sure which is an adventure and which is a tree or a boat.[1]

'Now I know he isn't Tortoise at all. But' – and then he scratched his head with his un-prickly paw – 'how do I know that this other is Tortoise?'

'But I *am* Tortoise,' said Slow-and-Solid. 'Your mother was quite right. She said that you were to scoop me out of my shell with your paw. Begin.'

'You didn't say she said that a minute ago,' said Painted Jaguar, sucking the prickles out of his paddy-paw. 'You said she said something quite different.'

'Well, suppose you say that I said that she said something quite different, I don't see that it makes any difference; because if she said what you said I said she said, it's just the same as if I said what she said she said. On the other hand, if you think she said that you were to uncoil me with a scoop, instead of pawing me into drops with a shell, I can't help that, can I?'

'But you said you wanted to be scooped out of your shell with my paw,' said Painted Jaguar.

'If you'll think again you'll find that I didn't say anything of the kind. I said that your mother said that you were to scoop me out of my shell,' said Slow-and-Solid.

'What will happen if I do?' said the Jaguar most sniffily and most cautious.

'I don't know, because I've never been scooped out of my shell before; but I tell you truly, if you want to see me swim away you've only got to drop me into the water.'

'I don't believe it,' said Painted Jaguar. 'You've mixed up all the things my mother told me to do with the things that you asked me whether I was sure that she didn't say, till I don't know whether I'm on my head or my painted tail; and now you come and tell me something I *can* understand, and it makes me more mixy than before. My mother told me that I was to drop one of you two into the water, and as you seem so anxious to be dropped I think you don't want to be dropped. So jump into the turbid Amazon and be quick about it.'

'I warn you that your Mummy won't be pleased. Don't tell her I didn't tell you,' said Slow-and-Solid.

'If you say another word about what my mother said – ' the Jaguar answered, but he had not finished the sentence before

Slow-and-Solid quietly dived into the turbid Amazon, swam under water for a long way, and came out on the bank where Stickly-Prickly was waiting for him.

'That was a very narrow escape,' said Stickly-Prickly. 'I don't like Painted Jaguar. What did you tell him that you were?'

'I told him truthfully that I was a truthful Tortoise, but he wouldn't believe it, and he made me jump into the river to see if I was, and I was, and he is surprised. Now he's gone to tell his Mummy. Listen to him!'

They could hear Painted Jaguar roaring up and down among the trees and the bushes by the side of the turbid Amazon, till his Mummy came.

'Son, son!' said his mother ever so many times, graciously waving her tail, 'what have you been doing that you shouldn't have done?'

'I tried to scoop something that said it wanted to be scooped out of its shell with my paw, and my paw is full of per-ickles,' said Painted Jaguar.

'Son, son!' said his mother ever so many times, graciously waving her tail, 'by the prickles in your paddy-paw I see that that must have been a Hedgehog. You should have dropped him into the water.'

'I did that to the other thing; he said he was a Tortoise, and I didn't believe him, and it was quite true, and he has dived under the turbid Amazon, and he won't come up again, and I haven't anything at all to eat, and I think we had better find lodgings somewhere else. They are too clever on the turbid Amazon for poor me!'

'Son, son!' said his mother ever so many times, graciously waving her tail, 'now attend to me and remember what I say. A Hedgehog curls himself up into a ball and his prickles stick out every which way at once. By this you may know the Hedgehog.'

'I don't like this old lady one little bit,' said Stickly-Prickly, under the shadow of a large leaf. 'I wonder what else she knows?'

'A Tortoise can't curl himself up,' Mother Jaguar went on, ever so many times, graciously waving her tail. 'He only draws his head and legs into his shell. By this you may know the Tortoise.'

'I don't like this old lady at all – at all,' said Slow-and-Solid Tortoise. 'Even Painted Jaguar can't forget those directions. It's a great pity that you can't swim, Stickly-Prickly.'

'Don't talk to me,' said Stickly-Prickly. 'Just think how much better it would be if you could curl up. This *is* a mess! Listen to Painted Jaguar.

Painted Jaguar was sitting on the banks of the turbid Amazon sucking prickles out of his paws and saying to himself:

> 'Can't curl, but can swim –
> Slow-Solid, that's him!
> Curls up, but can't swim –
> Stickly-Prickly, that's him!'

'He'll never forget that this month of Sundays,' said Stickly-Prickly. 'Hold up my chin, Slow-and-Solid. I'm going to try to learn to swim. It may be useful.'

'Excellent!' said Slow-and-Solid; and he held up Stickly-Prickly's chin, while Stickly-Prickly kicked in the waters of the turbid Amazon.

'You'll make a fine swimmer yet,' said Slow-and-Solid. 'Now, if you can unlace my back-plates a little, I'll see what I can do towards curling up. It may be useful.'

Stickly-Prickly helped to unlace Tortoise's back-plates, so that by twisting and straining Slow-and-Solid actually managed to curl up a tiddy wee bit.

'Excellent!' said Stickly-Prickly; 'but I shouldn't do any more just now. It's making you black in the face. Kindly lead me into the water once again and I'll practise that side-stroke which you say is so easy.' And so Stickly-Prickly practised, and Slow-and-Solid swam alongside.

'Excellent!' said Slow-and-Solid. 'A little more practice will make you a regular whale. Now, if I may trouble you to unlace my back and front plates two holes more, I'll try that fascinating bend that you say is so easy. Won't Painted Jaguar be surprised!'

'Excellent!' said Stickly-Prickly, all wet from the turbid

Amazon. 'I declare, I shouldn't know you from one of my own family. Two holes, I think, you said? A little more expression, please, and don't grunt quite so much, or Painted Jauguar may hear us. When you've finished, I want to try that long dive which you say is so easy. Won't Painted Jaguar be surprised!'

And so Stickly-Prickly dived, and Slow-and-Solid dived alongside.

'Excellent!' said Slow-and-Solid. 'A leetle more attention to holding your breath and you will be able to keep house at the bottom of the turbid Amazon. Now I'll try that exercise of wrapping my hind legs round my ears which you say is so peculiarly comfortable. Won't Painted Jaguar be surprised!'

'Excellent!' said Stickly-Prickly. 'But it's straining your back-plates a little. They are all overlapping now, instead of lying side by side.'

'Oh, that's the result of exercise,' said Slow-and-Solid. 'I've noticed that your prickles seem to be melting into one another, and that you're growing to look rather more like a pine-cone, and less like a chestnut-burr, than you used to.'

'Am I?' said Stickly-Prickly. 'That comes from my soaking in the water. Oh, won't Painted Jaguar be surprised!'

They went on with their exercises, each helping the other, till morning came; and when the sun was high they rested and dried themselves. Then they saw that they were both of them quite different from what they had been.

'Stickly-Prickly,' said Tortoise after breakfast, 'I am not what I was yesterday; but I think that I may yet amuse Painted Jaguar.'

'That was the very thing I was thinking just now,' said Stickly-Prickly. 'I think scales are a tremendous improvement on prickles – to say nothing of being able to swim. Oh, *won't* Painted Jaguar be surprised! Let's go and find him.'

By and by they found Painted Jaguar, still nursing his paddy-paw that had been hurt the night before. He was so astonished that he fell three times backward over his own painted tail without stopping.

'Good morning!' said Stickly-Prickly. 'And how is your dear gracious Mummy this morning?'

'She is quite well, thank you,' said Painted Jaguar; 'but you must forgive me if I do not at this precise moment recall your name.'

'That's unkind of you,' said Stickly-Prickly, 'seeing that this time yesterday you tried to scoop me out of my shell with your paw.'

'But you hadn't any shell. It was all prickles,' said Painted Jaguar. 'I know it was. Just look at my paw!'

'You told me to drop into the turbid Amazon and be drowned,' said Slow-Solid. 'Why are you so rude and forgetful today?'

'Don't you remember what your mother told you?' said Stickly-Prickly, –

> 'Can't curl, but can swim –
> Stickly-Prickly, that's him!
> Curls up, but can't swim –
> Slow-Solid, that's him!'

Then they both curled themselves up and rolled round and round Painted Jaguar till his eyes turned truly cart-wheels in his head.

Then he went to fetch his mother.

'Mother,' he said, 'there are two new animals in the woods today, and the one that you said, couldn't swim, swims, and the one that you said couldn't curl up, curls; and they've gone shares in their prickles, I think, because both of them are scaly all over, instead of one being smooth and the other very prickly; and, besides that, they are rolling round and round in circles, and I don't feel comfy.'

'Son, son!' said Mother Jaguar ever so many times, graciously waving her tail, 'a Hedgehog is a Hedgehog, and can't be anything but a Hedgehog; and a Tortoise is a Tortoise, and can never be anything else.'

'But it isn't a Hedgehog, and it isn't a Tortoise. It's a little bit of both, and I don't know its proper name.'

'Nonsense!' said Mother Jaguar. 'Everything has its proper name. I should call it "Armadillo" till I found out the real one. And I should leave it alone.'

The Beginning of the Armadilloes

So Painted Jaguar did as he was told, especially about leaving them alone; but the curious thing is that from that day to this, O Best Beloved, no one on the banks of the turbid Amazon has ever called Stickly-Prickly and Slow-and-Solid anything except Armadillo. There are Hedgehogs and Tortoises in other places, of course (there are some in my garden); but the real old and clever kind, with their scales lying lippety-lappety one over the other, like pine-cone scales, that lived on the banks of the turbid Amazon in the High and Far-Off Days, are always called Armadilloes, because they were so clever.

So *that*'s all right, Best Beloved. Do you see?

This is a picture of the whole story of the Jaguar and the Hedgehog and the Tortoise *and* the Armadillo all in a heap. It looks rather the same any way you turn it. The Tortoise is in the middle, learning how to bend, and that is why the shelly plates on his back are so spread apart. He is standing on the Hedgehog, who is waiting to learn how to swim. The Hedgehog is a Japanesy Hedgehog, because I couldn't find our own Hedgehogs in the garden when I wanted to draw them. (It was daytime, and they had gone to bed under the dahlias.) Painted Jaguar is looking over the edge, with his paddy-paw carefully tied up by his mother, because he pricked himself scooping the Hedgehog. He is much surprised to see what the Tortoise is doing, and his paw is hurting him. The snouty thing with the little eye that Painted Jaguar is trying to climb over is the Armadillo that the Tortoise and the Hedgehog are going to turn into when they have finished bending and swimming. It is all a magic picture, and that is one of the reasons why I haven't drawn the Jaguar's whiskers. The other reason was that he was so young that his whiskers had not grown. The Jaguar's pet name with his Mummy was Doffles.

I've never sailed the Amazon,
   I've never reached Brazil;
But the *Don* and *Magdalena*,
   They can go there when they will!

            Yes, weekly from Southampton,
            Great steamers, white and gold,[2]
            Go rolling down to Rio
            (Roll down – roll down to Rio!)
            And I'd like to roll to Rio
            Some day before I'm old!

I've never seen a Jaguar,
   Nor yet an Armadill –
O dilloing in his armour,
   And I s'pose I never will,

            Unless I go to Rio
            These wonders to behold –
            Roll down – roll down to Rio –
            Roll really down to Rio!
            Oh, I'd love to roll to Rio
            Some day before I'm old!

How the First Letter was Written

ONCE upon a most early time was a Neolithic man. He was not a Jute or an Angle, or even a Dravidian,[1] which he might well have been, Best Beloved, but never mind why. He was a Primitive, and he lived cavily in a Cave, and he wore very few clothes, and he couldn't read and he couldn't write and he didn't want to, and except when he was hungry he was quite happy. His name was Tegumai Bopsulai, and that means 'Man-who-does-not-put-his-foot-forward-in-a-hurry'; but we, O Best Beloved, will call him Tegumai, for short. And his wife's name was Teshumai Tewindrow, and that means 'Lady-who-asks-a-very-many-questions'; but we, O Best Beloved, will call her Teshumai, for short. And his little girl-daughter's name was Taffimai Metallumai, and that means 'Small-person-without-any-manners-who-ought-to-be-spanked'; but I'm going to call her Taffy. And she was Tegumai Bopsulai's Best Beloved and her own Mummy's Best Beloved, and she was not spanked half as much as was good for her; and they were all three very happy. As soon as Taffy could run about she went everywhere with her Daddy Tegumai, and sometimes they would not come home to the Cave till they were hungry, and then Teshumai Tewindrow would say, 'Where in the world have you two been to, to get so shocking dirty? Really, my Tegumai, you're no better than my Taffy.'

Now attend and listen!

One day Tegumai Bopsulai went down through the beaver-swamp to the Wagai river to spear carp-fish for dinner, and

Taffy went too. Tegumai's spear was made of wood with shark's teeth at the end, and before he had caught any fish at all he accidentally broke it clean across by jabbing it down too hard on the bottom of the river. They were miles and miles from home (of course they had their lunch with them in a little bag), and Tegumai had forgotten to bring any extra spears.

'Here's a pretty kettle of fish!' said Tegumai. 'It will take me half the day to mend this.'

'There's your big black spear at home,' said Taffy. 'Let me run back to the Cave and ask Mummy to give it me.'

'It's too far for your little fat legs,' said Tegumai. 'Besides, you might fall into the beaver-swamp and be drowned. We must make the best of a bad job.' He sat down and took out a little leather mendy-bag, full of reindeer-sinews and strips of leather, and lumps of bees-wax and resin, and began to mend the spear. Taffy sat down too, with her toes in the water and her chin in her hand, and thought very hard. Then she said:

'I say, Daddy, it's an awful nuisance that you and I don't know how to write, isn't it? If we did we could send a message for the new spear.'

'Taffy,' said Tegumai, 'how often have I told you not to use slang? "Awful" isn't a pretty word, – but it *would* be a convenience, now you mention it, if we could write home.'

Just then a Stranger-man came along the river, but he belonged to a far tribe, the Tewaras, and he did not understand one word of Tegumai's language. He stood on the bank and smiled at Taffy, because he had a little girl-daughter of his own at home. Tegumai drew a hank of deer-sinews from his mendy-bag and began to mend his spear.

'Come here,' said Taffy. 'Do you know where my Mummy lives?' And the Stranger-man said 'Um!' – being, as you know, a Tewara.

'Silly!' said Taffy, and she stamped her foot, because she saw a shoal of very big carp going up the river just when her Daddy couldn't use his spear.

'Don't bother grown-ups,' said Tegumai, so busy with his spear-mending that he did not turn round.

'I aren't,' said Taffy. 'I only want him to do what I want him to do, and he won't understand.'

'Then don't bother me,' said Tegumai, and he went on pulling and straining at the deer-sinews with his mouth full of loose ends. The Stranger-man – a genuine Tewara he was – sat down on the grass, and Taffy showed him what her Daddy was doing. The Stranger-man thought, 'This is a very wonderful child. She stamps her foot at me and she makes faces. She must be the daughter of that noble Chief who is so great that he won't take any notice of me.' So he smiled more politely than ever.

'Now,' said Taffy, 'I want you to go to my Mummy, because your legs are longer than mine, and you won't fall into the beaver-swamp, and ask for Daddy's other spear – the one with the black handle that hangs over our fireplace.'

The Stranger-man (*and* he was a Tewara) thought, 'This is a very, very wonderful child. She waves her arms and she shouts at me, but I don't understand a word of what she says. But if I don't do what she wants, I greatly fear that that haughty Chief, Man-who-turns-his-back-on-callers, will be angry.' He got up and twisted a big flat piece of bark off a birch-tree and gave it to Taffy. He did this, Best Beloved, to show that his heart was as white as the birch-bark and that he meant no harm; but Taffy didn't quite understand.

'Oh!' said she. 'Now I see! You want my Mummy's living address? Of course I can't write, but I can draw pictures if I've anything sharp to scratch with. Please lend me the shark's tooth off your necklace.'

The Stranger-man (and *he* was a Tewara) didn't say anything, so Taffy put up her little hand and pulled at the beautiful bead and seed and shark-tooth necklace round his neck.

The Stranger-man (and he *was* a Tewara) thought, 'This is a very, very, very wonderful child. The shark's tooth on my necklace is a magic shark's tooth, and I was always told that if anybody touched it without my leave they would immediately swell up or burst. But this child doesn't swell up or burst, and that important Chief, Man-who-attends-strictly-to-his-business, who has not yet taken any notice of me at all, doesn't seem

97

to be afraid that she will swell up or burst. I had better be more polite.'

So he gave Taffy the shark's tooth, and she lay down flat on her tummy with her legs in the air, like some people on the drawing-room floor when they want to draw pictures, and she said, 'Now I'll draw you some beautiful pictures! You can look over my shoulder, but you mustn't joggle. First I'll draw Daddy fishing. It isn't very like him; but Mummy will know, because I've drawn his spear all broken. Well, now I'll draw the other spear that he wants, the black-handled spear. It looks as if it was sticking in Daddy's back, but that's because the shark's tooth slipped and this piece of bark isn't big enough. That's the spear I want you to fetch; so I'll draw a picture of me myself 'splaining to you. My hair doesn't stand up like I've drawn, but it's easier to draw that way. Now I'll draw you. *I* think you're very nice really, but I can't make you pretty in the picture, so you mustn't be 'fended. Are you 'fended?'

The Stranger-man (and he was *a* Tewara) smiled. He thought, 'There must be a big battle going to be fought somewhere, and this extraordinary child, who takes my magic shark's tooth but who does not swell up or burst, is telling me to call all the great Chief's tribe to help him. He *is* a great Chief, or he would have noticed me.'

'Look,' said Taffy, drawing very hard and rather scratchily, 'now I've drawn you, and I've put the spear that Daddy wants into your hand, just to remind you that you're to bring it. Now I'll show you how to find Mummy's living-address. You go along till you come to two trees (those are trees), and then you go over a hill (that's a hill), and then you come into a beaver-swamp all full of beavers. I haven't put in all the beavers, because I can't draw beavers, but I've drawn their heads, and that's all you'll see of them when you cross the swamp. Mind you don't fall in! Then our Cave is just beyond the beaver-swamp. It isn't as high as the hills really, but I can't draw things very small. That's my Mummy outside. She is beautiful. She is the most beautifullest Mummy there ever was, but she won't be 'fended when she sees I've drawn her so plain. She'll be pleased of me because I can draw. Now, in case you forget, I've drawn the spear that Daddy wants *outside* our Cave. It's *inside* really, but you show the picture to my Mummy and she'll give it you. I've made her holding up her hands, because I know she'll be so pleased to see you. Isn't it a beautiful picture? And do you quite understand, or shall I 'splain again?'

The Stranger-man (and he was a *Tewara*) looked at the picture and nodded very hard. He said to himself, 'If I do not fetch this great Chief's tribe to help him, he will be slain by his enemies who are coming up on all sides with spears. Now I see why the great Chief pretended not to notice me! He feared that his enemies were hiding in the bushes and would see him deliver a message to me. Therefore he turned his back, and let the wise and wonderful child draw the terrible picture showing me his difficulties. I will away and get help for him from his tribe.' He did not even ask Taffy the road, but raced off into the bushes like the wind, with the birch-bark in his hand, and Taffy sat down most pleased.

Now this is the picture that Taffy had drawn for him!

'What have you been doing, Taffy?' said Tegumai. He had mended his spear and was carefully waving it to and fro.

'It's a little berangement of my own, Daddy dear,' said Taffy. 'If you won't ask me questions, you'll know all about it in a little time, and you'll be surprised. You don't know how surprised you'll be, Daddy! Promise you'll be surprised.'

'Very well,' said Tegumai, and went on fishing.

The Stranger-man – did you know he was a Tewara? – hurried away with the picture and ran for some miles, till quite by accident he found Teshumai Tewindrow at the door of her Cave, talking to some other Neolithic ladies who had come in to a Primitive lunch. Taffy was very like Teshumai, specially about the upper part of the face and the eyes, so the Stranger-man – always a pure Tewara – smiled politely and handed Teshumai the birch-bark. He had run hard, so that he panted, and his legs were scratched with brambles, but he still tried to be polite.

As soon as Teshumai saw the picture she screamed like anything and flew at the Stranger-man. The other Neolithic ladies at once knocked him down and sat on him in a long line of six, while Teshumai pulled his hair. 'It's as plain as the nose on this Stranger-man's face,' she said. 'He has stuck my Tegumai all full of spears, and frightened poor Taffy so that her hair stands all on end; and not content with that, he brings me a horrid picture of how it was done. Look!' She showed the picture to all the Neolithic ladies sitting patiently on the Stranger-man. 'Here is my Tegumai with his arm broken; here is a spear sticking into his back; here is a man with a spear ready to throw; here is another man throwing a spear from a Cave, and here are a whole pack of people' (they were Taffy's beavers really, but they did look rather like people) 'coming up behind Tegumai. Isn't it shocking!'

'Most shocking!' said the Neolithic ladies, and they filled the Stranger-man's hair with mud (at which he was surprised), and they beat upon the Reverberating Tribal Drums, and called together all the chiefs of the Tribe of Tegumai, with their Hetmans and Dolmans, all Neguses, Woons, and Akhoonds of the organization, in addition to the Warlocks, Angekoks, Jujumen, Bonzes,[2] and the rest, who decided that before they chopped the Stranger-man's head off he should instantly lead them down to the river and show them where he had hidden poor Taffy.

By this time the Stranger-man (in spite of being a Tewara) was really annoyed. They had filled his hair quite solid with mud; they had rolled him up and down on knobby pebbles; they had sat upon him in a long line of six; they had thumped him and bumped him till he could hardly breathe; and though he did not understand their language, he was almost sure that the names the Neolithic ladies called him were not ladylike. However, he said nothing till all the Tribe of Tegumai were assembled, and then he led them back to the bank of the Wagai river, and there they found Taffy making daisy-chains, and Tegumai carefully spearing small carp with his mended spear.

'Well, you *have* been quick!' said Taffy. 'But why did you bring so many people? Daddy dear, this is my surprise. *Are* you surprised, Daddy?'

'Very,' said Tegumai; 'but it has ruined all my fishing for the day. Why, the whole dear, kind, nice, clean, quiet Tribe is here, Taffy.'

And so they were. First of all walked Teshumai Tewindrow and the Neolithic ladies, tightly holding on to the Stranger-man, whose hair was full of mud (although he was a Tewara). Behind them came the Head Chief, the Vice-Chief, the Deputy and Assistant Chiefs (all armed to the upper teeth), the Hetmens and Heads of Hundreds,[3] Platoffs[4] with their Platoons, and Dolmans with their Detachments; Woons, Neguses, and Akhoonds ranking in the rear (still armed to the teeth). Behind them was the Tribe in hierarchical order, from owners of four caves (one for each season), a private reindeer-run, and two salmon-leaps, to feudal and prognathous Villeins,[5] semi-entitled to half a bearskin of winter nights, seven yards from the fire, and adscript serfs,[6] holding the reversion of a scraped marrow-bone under heriot[7] (Aren't those beautiful words, Best Beloved?). They were all there, prancing and shouting, and they frightened every fish for twenty miles, and Tegumai thanked them in a fluid Neolithic oration.

Then Teshumai Tewindrow ran down and kissed and

hugged Taffy very much indeed; but the Head Chief of the Tribe of Tegumai took Tegumai by the top-knot feathers and shook him severely.

'Explain! Explain! Explain!' cried all the Tribe of Tegumai.

'Goodness' sakes alive!' said Tegumai. 'Let go of my top-knot. Can't a man break his carp-spear without the whole countryside descending on him? You're a very interfering people.'

'I don't believe you've brought my Daddy's black-handled spear after all,' said Taffy. 'And what *are* you doing to my nice Stranger-man?'

They were thumping him by twos and threes and tens till his eyes turned round and round. He could only gasp and point at Taffy.

'Where are the bad people who speared you, my darling?' said Teshumai Tewindrow.

'There weren't any,' said Tegumai. 'My only visitor this morning was the poor fellow that you are trying to choke. Aren't you well, or are you ill, O Tribe of Tegumai?'

'He came with a horrible picture,' said the Head Chief, – 'a picture that showed you were full of spears.'

'Er – um – P'raps I'd better 'splain that I gave him that picture,' said Taffy, but she did not feel quite comfy.

'You!' said the Tribe of Tegumai all together. 'Small-person-with-no-manners-who-ought-to-be-spanked! You?'

'Taffy, dear, I'm afraid we're in for a little trouble,' said her Daddy, and put his arm round her, so she didn't care.

'Explain! Explain! Explain!' said the Head Chief of the Tribe of Tegumai, and he hopped on one foot.

'I wanted the Stranger-man to fetch Daddy's spear, so I drawded it,' said Taffy. 'There wasn't lots of spears. There was only one spear. I drawded it three times to make sure. I couldn't help it looking as if it stuck into Daddy's head – there wasn't room on the birch-bark; and those things that Mummy called bad people are my beavers. I drawded them to show him the way through the swamp; and I drawded Mummy at the mouth of the Cave looking pleased because he is a nice Stranger-man, and *I* think you are just the stupidest people in the world,' said

Taffy. 'He is a very nice man. Why have you filled his hair with mud? Wash him!'

Nobody said anything at all for a long time, till the Head Chief laughed; then the Stranger-man (who was at least a Tewara) laughed; then Tegumai laughed till he fell down flat on the bank; then all the Tribe laughed more and worse and louder. The only people who did not laugh were Teshumai Tewindrow and all the Neolithic ladies. They were very polite to all their husbands, and said 'Idiot!' ever so often.

Then the Head Chief of the Tribe of Tegumai cried and said and sang, 'O Small-person-without-any-manners-who-ought-to-be-spanked, you've hit upon a great invention!'

'I didn't intend to; I only wanted Daddy's black-handled spear,' said Taffy.

'Never mind. It *is* a great invention, and some day men will call it writing. At present it is only pictures, and, as we have seen today, pictures are not always properly understood. But a time will come, O Babe of Tegumai, when we shall make letters – all twenty-six of 'em, – and when we shall be able to read as well as to write, and then we shall always say exactly what we mean without any mistakes. Let the Neolithic ladies wash the mud out of the stranger's hair!'

'I shall be glad of that,' said Taffy, 'because after all, though you've brought every single other spear in the Tribe of Tegumai, you've forgotten my Daddy's black-handled spear.'

Then the Head Chief cried and said and sang, 'Taffy dear, the next time you write a picture-letter, you'd better send a man who can talk our language with it, to explain what it means. I don't mind it myself, because I am a Head Chief, but it's very bad for the rest of the Tribe of Tegumai, and, as you can see, it surprises the stranger.'

Then they adopted the Stranger-man (a genuine Tewara of Tewar) into the Tribe of Tegumai, because he was a gentleman and did not make a fuss about the mud that the Neolithic ladies had put into his hair. But from that day to this (and I suppose it is all Taffy's fault), very few little girls have ever liked learning to read or write. Most of them prefer to draw pictures and play about with their Daddies – just like Taffy.

This is the story of Taffimai Metallumai carved on an old tusk a very long time ago by the Ancient Peoples. If you read my story, or have it read to you, you can see how it is all told out on the tusk. The tusk was part of an old tribal trumpet that belonged to the Tribe of Tegumai. The pictures were scratched on it with a nail or something, and then the scratches were filled up with black wax, but all the dividing lines and the five little rounds at the bottom were filled with red wax. When it was new there was a sort of network of beads and shells and precious stones at one end of it; but now that has been broken and lost – all except the little bit that you see. The letters round the tusk are magic – Runic magic,[8] – and if you can read them you will find out something rather new. The tusk is of ivory – very yellow and scratched. It is two feet long and two feet round, and weighs eleven pounds nine ounces.

There runs a road by Merrow Down –
    A grassy track today it is –
An hour out of Guildford town,
    Above the river Wey it is.

Here, when they heard the horse-bells ring,
    The ancient Britons dressed and rode
To watch the dark Phœnicians bring
    Their goods along the Western Road.

And here, or hereabouts, they met
    To hold their racial talks and such –
To barter beads for Whitby jet,
    And tin for gay shell torques and such.

But long and long before that time
    (When bison used to roam on it)
Did Taffy and her Daddy climb
    That down, and had their home on it.

Then beavers built in Broadstonebrook
    And made a swamp where Bramley stands;
And bears from Shere would come and look
    For Taffimai where Shamley stands.

The Wey, that Taffy called Wagai,
    Was more than six times bigger then;
And all the Tribe of Tegumai
    They cut a noble figure then!

How the Alphabet was Made[1]

HE week after Taffimai Metal-lumai (we will still call her Taffy, Best Beloved) made that little mistake about her Daddy's spear and the Stranger-man and the picture-letter and all, she went carp-fishing again with her Daddy. Her Mummy wanted her to stay at home and help hang up hides to dry on the big drying-poles outside their Neolithic Cave, but Taffy slipped away down to her Daddy quite early, and they fished. Presently she began to giggle, and her Daddy said, 'Don't be silly, child.'

'But wasn't it inciting!' said Taffy. 'Don't you remember how the Head Chief puffed out his cheeks, and how funny the nice Stranger-man looked with the mud in his hair?'

'Well do I,' said Tegumai. 'I had to pay two deerskins – soft ones with fringes – to the Stranger-man for the things we did to him.'

'*We* didn't do anything,' said Taffy. 'It was Mummy and the other Neolithic ladies – and the mud.'

'We won't talk about that,' said her Daddy. 'Let's have lunch.'

Taffy took a marrow-bone and sat mousy-quiet for ten whole minutes, while her Daddy scratched on pieces of birch-bark with a shark's tooth. Then she said, 'Daddy, I've thinked of a secret surprise. You make a noise – any sort of noise.'

'Ah!' said Tegumai. 'Will that do to begin with?'

'Yes,' said Taffy. 'You look just like a carp-fish with its mouth open. Say it again, please.'

'Ah! ah! ah!' said her Daddy. 'Don't be rude, my daughter.'

'I'm not meaning rude, really and truly,' said Taffy. 'It's part of my secret-surprise-think. *Do* say *ah*, Daddy, and keep your mouth open at the end, and lend me that tooth. I'm going to draw a carp-fish's mouth wide-open.'

'What for?' said her Daddy.

'Don't you see?' said Taffy, scratching away on the bark. 'That will be our little secret s'prise. When I draw a carp-fish with his mouth open in the smoke at the back of our Cave – if Mummy doesn't mind – it will remind you of that ah-noise. Then we can play that it was me jumped out of the dark and s'prised you with that noise – same as I did in the beaver-swamp last winter.'

'Really?' said her Daddy, in the voice that grown-ups use when they are truly attending. 'Go on, Taffy.'

'Oh, bother!' she said. 'I can't draw all of a carp-fish, but I can draw something that means a carp-fish's mouth. Don't you know how they stand on their heads rooting in the mud? Well, here's a pretence carp-fish (we can play that the rest of him is drawn). Here's just his mouth, and that means *ah*.' And she drew this. (1.)

'That's not bad,' said Tegumai, and scratched on his own piece of bark for himself; 'but you've forgotten the feeler that hangs across his mouth.'

'But I can't draw, Daddy.'

 'You needn't draw anything of him except just the opening of his mouth and the feeler across. Then we'll know he's a carp-fish, 'cause the perches and trouts haven't got feelers. Look here, Taffy.' And he drew this. (2.)

'Now I'll copy it,' said Taffy. 'Will you understand *this* when you see it?' And she drew this. (3.)

'Perfectly,' said her Daddy. 'And I'll be quite as s'prised when I see it anywhere, as if you had jumped out from behind a tree and said "Ah!"'

'Now, make another noise,' said Taffy, very proud.

'Yah!' said her Daddy, very loud.

'H'm,' said Taffy. 'That's a mixy noise. The end part is *ah*-carp-fish-mouth; but what can we do about the front part? *Yer-yer-yer* and *ah! Ya!*'

'It's very like the carp-fish-mouth noise. Let's draw another bit of the carp-fish and join 'em,' said her Daddy. *He* was quite incited too.

'No. If they're joined, I'll forget. Draw it separate. Draw his tail. If he's standing on his head the tail will come first. 'Sides, I think I can draw tails easiest,' said Taffy.

'A good notion,' said Tegumai. 'Here's a carp-fish tail for the *yer*-noise.' And he drew this. (4.)

4

'I'll try now,' said Taffy. ''Member I can't draw like you, Daddy. Will it do if I just draw the split part of the tail, and a sticky-down line for where it joins?' And she drew this (5.)

Her Daddy nodded, and his eyes were shiny bright with 'citement.

5

'That's beautiful,' she said. 'Now, make another noise, Daddy.'

'Oh!' said her Daddy, very loud.

'That's quite easy,' said Taffy. 'You make your mouth all round like an egg or a stone. So an egg or a stone will do for that.'

'You can't always find eggs or stones. We'll have to scratch a round something like one.' And he drew this. (6.)

6

'My gracious!' said Taffy, 'what a lot of noise-pictures we've made, – carp-mouth, carp-tail, and egg! Now, make another noise, Daddy.'

'Ssh!' said her Daddy, and frowned to himself, but Taffy was too incited to notice.

'That's quite easy,' she said, scratching on the bark.

'Eh, what?' said her Daddy. 'I meant I was thinking, and didn't want to be disturbed.'

'It's a noise, just the same. It's the noise a snake makes, Daddy, when it is thinking and doesn't want to be disturbed. Let's make the *ssh*-noise a snake. Will this do?' And she drew this. (7.)

'There,' she said. 'That's another s'prise-secret. When you draw a hissy-snake by the door of your little back-cave where you mend the spears, I'll know you're thinking hard; and I'll come in most mousy-quiet. And if you draw it on a tree by the river when you're fishing, I'll know you want me to walk most *most* mousy-quiet, so as not to shake the banks.'

'Perfectly true,' said Tegumai. 'And there's more in this game than you think. Taffy, dear, I've a notion that your Daddy's daughter has hit upon the finest thing that there ever was since the Tribe of Tegumai took to using shark's teeth instead of flints for their spear-heads. I believe we've found out *the* big secret of the world.'

'Why?' said Taffy, and her eyes shone too with incitement.

'I'll show,' said her Daddy. 'What's water in the Tegumai language?'

'*Ya*, of course, and it means river too – like Wagai-*ya* – the Wagai river.'

'What is bad water that gives you fever if you drink it – black water – swamp-water?'

'*Yo*, of course.'

'Now look,' said her Daddy. 'S'pose you saw this scratched by the side of a pool in the beaver-swamp?' And he drew this. (8.)

'Carp-tail and round egg. Two noises mixed! *Yo*, bad water,' said Taffy. ''Course I wouldn't drink that water because I'd know you said it was bad.'

'But I needn't be near the water at all. I might be miles away, hunting, and still – '

'And *still* it would be just the same as if you stood there and said, "G'way, Taffy, or you'll get fever." All that in a carp-fish-tail and a round egg! O Daddy, we must tell Mummy, quick!' and Taffy danced all round him.

'Not yet,' said Tegumai; 'not till we've gone a little further.

9

Let's see. *Yo* is bad water, but *so* is food cooked on the fire, isn't it?' And he drew this. (9.)

'Yes. Snake and egg,' said Taffy. 'So that means dinner's ready. If you saw that scratched on a tree you'd know it was time to come to the Cave. So'd I.'

'My Winkie!' said Tegumai. 'That's true too. But wait a minute. I see a difficulty. *So* means "come and have dinner," but *sho* means the drying-poles where we hang our hides.'

'Horrid old drying-poles!' said Taffy. 'I hate helping to hang heavy, hot, hairy hides on them. If you drew the snake and egg, and I thought it meant dinner, and I came in from the wood and found that it meant I was to help Mummy hand the hides on the drying-poles, what *would* I do?'

'You'd be cross. So'd Mummy. We must make a new picture for *sho*. We must draw a spotty snake that hisses *sh-sh*, and we'll play that the plain snake only hisses *ssss*.'

'I couldn't be sure how to put in the spots,' said Taffy. 'And p'raps if *you* were in a hurry you might leave them out, and I'd think it was *so* when it was *sho*, and then Mummy would catch me just the same. *No!* I think we'd better draw a picture of the horrid high drying-poles their very selves, and make *quite* sure. I'll put 'em in just after the hissy-snake. Look!' And she drew this. (10.)

'P'raps that's safest. It's very like our drying-poles, anyhow,' said her Daddy, laughing. 'Now I'll make a new noise with a snake and drying-pole sound in it. I'll say *shi*. That's Tegumai for spear, Taffy.' And he laughed.

'Don't make fun of me,' said Taffy, as she thought of her picture-letter and the mud in the Stranger-man's hair. '*You* draw it, Daddy.'

'We won't have beavers or hills this time, eh?' said her Daddy. 'I'll just draw a straight line for my spear.' And he drew this. (11.)

'Even Mummy couldn't mistake that for me being killed.'

'*Please* don't, Daddy. It makes me uncomfy. Do some more noises. We're getting on beautifully.'

'Er-hm!' said Tegumai, looking up. 'We'll say *shu*. That means sky.'

Taffy drew the snake and the drying-pole. Then she stopped. 'We must make a new picture for that end sound, mustn't we?'

'*Shu-shu-u-u-u!*' said her Daddy. 'Why, it's just like the round-egg-sound made thin.'

'Then s'pose we draw a thin round egg, and pretend it's a frog that hasn't eaten anything for years.'

'N-no,' said her Daddy. 'If we drew that in a hurry we might mistake it for the round egg itself. *Shu-shu-shu!* I'll tell you what we'll do. We'll open a little hole at the end of the round egg to show how the O-noise runs out all thin, *ooo-oo-oo*. Like this.' And he drew this. (12.)

12

'Oh, that's lovely! Much better than a thin frog. Go on,' said Taffy, using her shark's tooth.

Her Daddy went on drawing, and his hand shook with incitement. He went on till he had drawn this. (13.)

13

'Don't look up, Taffy,' he said. 'Try if you can make out what that means in the Tegumai language. If you can, we've found the Secret.'

'Snake – pole – broken-egg – carp-tail and carp-mouth,' said Taffy. '*Shu-ya*. Sky-water rain.' Just then a drop fell on her hand, for the day had clouded over. 'Why, Daddy, it's raining. Was *that* what you meant to tell me?'

'Of course,' said her Daddy. 'And I told it you without saying a word, didn't I?'

'Well, I *think* I would have known it in a minute, but that raindrop made me quite sure. I'll always remember now. *Shu-ya* means rain, or "it is going to rain". Why, Daddy!' She got up and danced round him. 'S'pose you went out before I was awake, and drawed *shu-ya* in the smoke on the wall, I'd know it was going to rain and I'd take my beaver-skin hood. Wouldn't Mummy be surprised!'

Tegumai got up and danced. (Daddies didn't mind doing those things in those days.) 'More than that! More than that!' he said. 'S'pose I wanted to tell you it wasn't going to rain much and you must come down to the river, what would we draw? Say the words in Tegumai-talk first.'

'*Shu-ya-las, ya maru*. (Sky-water ending. River come to.) *What* a lot of new sounds! *I* don't see how we can draw them.'

'But I do – but I do!' said Tegumai. 'Just attend a minute, Taffy, and we won't do any more today. We've got *shu-ya* all right, haven't we? but this *las* is a teaser. *La-la-la!*' and he waved his shark-tooth.

'There's the hissy-snake at the end and the carp-mouth before the snake – *as-as-as*. We only want *la-la*,' said Taffy.

'I know it, but we have to make *la-la*. And we're the first people in all the world who've ever tried to do it, Taffimai!'

'Well,' said Taffy, yawning, for she was rather tired. '*Las* means breaking or finishing as well as ending, doesn't it?'

'So it does,' said Tegumai. '*Ya-las* means that there's no water in the tank for Mummy to cook with – just when I'm going hunting, too.'

'And *shi-las* means that your spear is broken. If I'd only thought of *that* instead of drawing silly beaver-pictures for the Stranger-man!'

'*La! La! La!*' said Tegumai, waving his stick and frowning. 'Oh, bother!'

'I could have drawn *shi* quite easily,' Taffy went on. 'Then I'd have drawn your spear all broken – this way!' And she drew. (14.)

'The very thing,' said Tegumai. 'That's *la* all over. It isn't like any of the other marks, either.' And he drew this. (15.)

'Now for *ya*. Oh, we've done that before. Now for *maru*.

Mum-mum-mum. Mum shuts one's mouth up, doesn't it? We'll draw a shut mouth like this.' And he drew. (16.)

'Then the carp-mouth open. That makes *Ma-ma-ma!* But what about this *rrrrr*-thing, Taffy?'

'It sounds all rough and edgy, like your shark-tooth saw when you're cutting out a plank for the canoe,' said Taffy.

'You mean all sharp at the edges, like this?' said Tegumai. And he drew. (17.)

''Xactly,' said Taffy. 'But we don't want all those teeth: only put two.'

17

'I'll only put in one,' said Tegumai. 'If this game of ours is going to be what I think it will, the easier we make our sound-pictures the better for everybody.' And he drew. (18.)

'*Now* we've got it,' said Tegumai, standing on one leg. 'I'll draw 'em all in a string like fish.'

18

'Hadn't we better put a little bit of stick or something between each word, so's they won't rub up against each other and jostle, same as if they were carps?'

'Oh, I'll leave a space for that,' said her Daddy. And very incitedly he drew them all without stopping, on a big new bit of birch-bark. (19.)

19

'*Shu-ya-las ya-maru,*' said Taffy, reading it out sound by sound.

'That's enough for today,' said Tegumai. 'Besides, you're getting tired, Taffy. Never mind, dear. We'll finish it all to-morrow, and then we'll be remembered for years and years after the biggest trees you can see are all chopped up for firewood.'

So they went home, and all that evening Tegumai sat on one side of the fire and Taffy on the other, drawing *ya's* and *yo's* and *shu's* and *shi's* in the smoke on the wall and giggling together till her Mummy said, 'Really, Tegumai, you're worse than my Taffy.'

'Please don't mind,' said Taffy. 'It's only our secret-s'prise, Mummy, dear, and we'll tell you all about it the very minute it's done; but *please* don't ask me what it is now, or else I'll have to tell.'

So her Mummy most carefully didn't; and bright and early next morning Tegumai went down to the river to think about new sound-pictures, and when Taffy got up she saw *Ya-las* (water is ending or running out) chalked on the side of the big stone water-tank, outside the Cave.

'Um,' said Taffy. 'These picture-sounds are rather a bother! Daddy's just as good as come here himself and told me to get more water for Mummy to cook with.' She went to the spring at the back of the house and filled the tank from a bark bucket, and then she ran down to the river and pulled her Daddy's left ear – the one that belonged to her to pull when she was good.

'Now come along and we'll draw all the left-over sound-pictures,' said her Daddy, and they had a most inciting day of it, and a beautiful lunch in the middle, and two games of romps. When they came to T, Taffy said that as her name, and her Daddy's, and her Mummy's all began with that sound, they should draw a sort of family group of themselves holding hands. That was all very well to draw once or twice; but when it came to drawing it six or seven times, Taffy and Tegumai drew it scratchier and scratchier, till at last the T-sound was only a thin long Tegumai with his arms out to hold Taffy and Teshu-mai. You can see from these three pictures partly how it happened. (20, 21, 22.)

Many of the other pictures were much too beautiful to begin with, especially before lunch; but as they were drawn over and

20   21   22   23

over again on birch-bark, they became plainer and easier, till at last even Tegumai said he could find no fault with them. They

turned the hissy-snake the other way round for the Z-sound, to
show it was hissing backwards in a soft and gentle way (23); and
they just made a twiddle for E, because it came into the pictures
so often (24); and they drew pictures of the sacred Beaver of

24   25   26   27

the Tegumais for the B-sound (25, 26, 27, 28); and because it
was a nasty, nosy noise, they just drew noses for the N-sound,
till they were tired (29); and they drew a picture of the big lake-
pike's mouth for the greedy Ga-sound (30); and they drew the

28   29   30

pike's mouth again with a spear behind it for the scratchy, hurty
Ka-sound (31); and they drew pictures of a little bit of the
winding Wagai river for the nice windy-windy Wa-sound (32,
33); and so on and so forth and so following till they had done
and drawn all the sound-pictures that they wanted, and there
was the Alphabet, all complete.

31   32   33

And after thousands and thousands and thousands of years,
and after Hieroglyphics, and Demotics, and Nilotics, and
Cryptics, and Cufics, and Runics, and Dorics, and Ionics,[2] and

all sorts of other ricks and tricks (because the Woons, and the Neguses, and the Akhoonds, and the Repositories of Tradition would never leave a good thing alone when they saw it), the fine old easy, understandable Alphabet – A, B, C, D, E, and the rest of 'em – got back into its proper shape again for all Best Beloveds to learn when they are old enough.

But *I* remember Tegumai Bopsulai, and Taffimai Metallumai and Teshumai Tewindrow, her dear Mummy, and all the days gone by. And it was so – just so – a long time ago – on the banks of the big Wagai!

One of the first things that Tegumai Bopsulai did after
Taffy and he had made the Alphabet was to make a magic
Alphabet-necklace of all the letters, so that it could be
put in the Temple of Tegumai and kept for ever and ever.
All the Tribe of Tegumai brought their most precious
beads and beautiful things, and Taffy and Tegumai
spent five whole years getting the necklace in order. This
is a picture of the magic Alphabet-necklace. The string
was made of the finest and strongest reindeer-sinew,
bound round with thin copper wire.

Beginning at the top, the first bead is an old silver one
that belonged to the Head Priest of the Tribe of Tegumai; then come three black mussel-pearls; next is a clay
bead (blue and grey); next a nubbly gold bead sent as a
present by a tribe who got it from Africa (but it must have
been Indian really); the next is a long flat-sided glass
bead from Africa (the Tribe of Tegumai took it in a
fight); then come two clay beads (white and green), with
dots on one, and dots and bands on the other; next are
three rather chipped amber beads; then three clay beads
(red and white), two with dots, and the big one in the
middle with a toothed pattern. Then the letters begin,
and between each letter is a little whitish clay bead with
the letter repeated small. Here are the letters:

A is scratched on a tooth – an elk-tush, I think.
B is the Sacred Beaver of Tegumai on a bit of old
   ivory.
C is a pearly oyster-shell – inside front.
D must be a sort of mussel-shell – outside front.
E is a twist of silver wire.
F is broken, but what remains of it is a bit of stag's
   horn.
G is painted black on a piece of wood. (The bead after
   G is a small shell, and not a clay bead. I don't know
   why they did that.)
H is a kind of big brown cowrie-shell.
I   is the inside part of a long shell ground down by

hand. (It took Tegumai three months to grind it down.)

J is a fish-hook in mother-of-pearl.

L is the broken spear in silver. (K ought to follow J, of course; but the necklace was broken once and they mended it wrong.)

K is a thin slice of bone scratched and rubbed in black.

M is on a pale grey shell.

N is a piece of what is called porphyry with a nose scratched on it. (Tegumai spent five months polishing this stone.)

O is a piece of oyster-shell with a hole in the middle.

P and Q are missing. They were lost, a long time ago, in a great war, and the tribe mended the necklace with the dried rattles of a rattlesnake, but no one ever found P and Q. That is how the saying began, 'You must mind your P's and Q's.'

R is, of course, just a shark's tooth.

S is a little silver snake.

T is the end of a small bone, polished brown and shiny.

U is another piece of oyster-shell.

W is a twisty piece of mother-of-pearl that they found inside a big mother-of-pearl shell, and sawed off with a wire dipped in sand and water. It took Taffy a month and a half to polish it and drill the holes.

X is silver wire joined in the middle with a raw garnet. (Taffy found the garnet.)

Y is the carp's tail in ivory.

Z is a bell-shaped piece of agate marked with Z-shaped stripes. They made the Z-snake out of one of the stripes by picking out the soft stone and rubbing in red sand and bees-wax. Just in the mouth of the bell you see the clay bead repeating the Z-letter.

These are all the letters.

The next bead is a small round greeny lump of copper ore; the next is a lump of rough turquoise; the next is a rough gold nugget (what they call water-gold); the next is a melon-shaped clay bead (white with green spots). Then come four flat ivory pieces, with dots on them rather like dominoes; then come three stone beads, very badly worn; then two soft iron beads with rust-holes at the edges (they must have been magic, because they look very common); and last is a very very old African bead, like glass – blue, red, white, black, and yellow. Then comes the loop to slip over the big silver button at the other end, and that is all.

I have copied the necklace very carefully. It weighs one pound seven and a half ounces. The black squiggle behind is only put in to make the beads and things look better.

Of all the Tribe of Tegumai
    Who cut that figure, none remain, –
On Merrow Down the cuckoos cry –
    The silence and the sun remain.

But as the faithful years return
    And hearts unwounded sing again,
Comes Taffy dancing through the fern
    To lead the Surrey spring again.

Her brows are bound with bracken-fronds,
    And golden elf-locks fly above;
Her eyes are bright as diamonds
    And bluer than the skies above.

In moccasins and deer-skin cloak,
    Unfearing, free and fair she flits,
And lights her little damp-wood smoke
    To show her Daddy where she flits.

For far – oh, very far behind,
    So far she cannot call to him,
Comes Tegumai alone to find
    The daughter that was all to him.

EFORE the High and Far-Off Times, O my Best Beloved, came the Time of the Very Beginnings; and that was in the days when the Eldest Magician was getting Things ready. First he got the Earth ready; then he got the Sea ready; and then he told all the Animals that they could come out and play. And the Animals said, 'O Eldest Magician, what shall we play at?' and he said, 'I will show you.' He took the Elephant – All-the-Elephant-there-was – and said, 'Play at being an Elephant,' and All-the-Elephant-there-was played. He took the Beaver – All-the-Beaver-there-was – and said, 'Play at being a Beaver,' and All-the-Beaver-there-was played. He took the Cow – All-the-Cow-there-was – and said, 'Play at being a Cow,' and All-the-Cow-there-was played. He took the Turtle – All-the-Turtle-there-was – and said, 'Play at being a Turtle,' and All-the-Turtle-there-was played. One by one he took all the beasts and birds and fishes and told them what to play at.

But towards evening, when people and things grow restless and tired, there came up the Man (With his own little girl-daughter?) – Yes, with his own best-beloved little girl-daughter sitting upon his shoulder, and he said, 'What is this play, Eldest Magician?' And the Eldest Magician said, 'Ho, Son of Adam, this is the play of the Very Beginning; but you are too wise for this play.' And the Man saluted and said, 'Yes, I am too wise for this play; but see that you make all the Animals obedient to me.'

Now, while the two were talking together, Pau Amma the Crab, who was next in the game, scuttled off sideways and stepped into the sea, saying to himself, 'I will play my play alone in the deep waters, and I will never be obedient to this son of Adam.' Nobody saw him go away except the little girl-daughter where she leaned on the Man's shoulder. And the play went on till there were no more Animals left without orders; and the Eldest Magician wiped the fine dust off his hands and walked about the world to see how the Animals were playing.

He went North, Best Beloved, and he found All-the-Elephant-there-was digging with his tusks and stamping with his feet in the nice new clean earth that had been made ready for him.

'*Kun?*' said All-the-Elephant-there-was, meaning, 'Is this right?'

'*Payah kun,*' said the Eldest Magician, meaning, 'That is quite right'; and he breathed upon the great rocks and lumps of earth that All-the-Elephant-there-was had thrown up, and they became the great Himalayan Mountains, and you can look them out on the map.

He went East, and he found All-the-Cow-there-was feeding in the field that had been made ready for her, and she licked her tongue round a whole forest at a time, and swallowed it and sat down to chew her cud.

'*Kun?*' said All-the-Cow-there-was.

'*Payah kun,*' said the Eldest Magician; and he breathed upon the bare patch where she had eaten, and upon the place where she had sat down, and one became the great Indian Desert, and the other became the Desert of Sahara, and you can look them out on the map.

He went West, and he found All-the-Beaver-there-was making a beaver-dam across the mouths of broad rivers that had been got ready for him.

'*Kun?*' said All-the-Beaver-there-was.

'*Payah kun,*' said the Eldest Magician; and he breathed upon the fallen trees and the still water, and they became the Everglades in Florida, and you may look them out on the map.

Then he went South and found All-the-Turtle-there-was scratching with his flippers in the sand that had been got ready for him, and the sand and the rocks whirled through the air and fell far off into the sea.

'*Kun?*' said All-the-Turtle-there-was.

'*Payah kun,*' said the Eldest Magician; and he breathed upon the sand and the rocks, where they had fallen in the sea, and they became the most beautiful islands of Borneo, Celebes, Sumatra, Java, and the rest of the Malay Archipelago, and you can look *them* out on the map

By and by the Eldest Magician met the Man on the banks of the Perak River, and said, 'Ho! Son of Adam, are all the Animals obedient to you?'

'Yes,' said the Man.

'Is all the Earth obedient to you?'

'Yes,' said the Man.

'Is all the Sea obedient to you?'

'No,' said the Man. 'Once a day and once a night the Sea runs up the Perak River and drives the sweet-water back into the forest, so that my house is made wet; once a day and once a night it runs down the river and draws all the water after it, so that there is nothing left but mud, and my canoe is upset. Is that the play you told it to play?'

'No,' said the Eldest Magician. 'That is a new and a bad play.'

'Look!' said the Man, and as he spoke the great Sea came up the mouth of the Perak River, driving the river backwards till it overflowed all the dark forests for miles and miles, and flooded the Man's house.

'This is wrong. Launch your canoe and we will find out who is playing with the Sea,' said the Eldest Magician. They stepped into the canoe; the little girl-daughter came with them; and the Man took his *kris* – a curving, wavy dagger with a blade like a flame, – and they pushed out on the Perak River. Then the Sea began to run back and back, and the canoe was sucked out of the mouth of the Perak River,[1] past Selangor, past Malacca,[2] past Singapore, out and out to the Island of Bintang,[3] as though it had been pulled by a string.

This is a picture of Pau Amma the Crab running away while the Eldest Magician was talking to the Man and his Little Girl-Daughter. The Eldest Magician is sitting on his magic throne, wrapped up in his Magic Cloud. The three flowers in front of him are the three Magic Flowers. On the top of the hill you can see All-the-Elephant-there-was, and All-the-Cow-there-was, and All-the-Turtle-there-was going off to play as the Eldest Magician told them. The Cow has a hump, because she was All-the-Cow-there-was; so she had to have all there was for all the cows that were made afterwards. Under the hill there are Animals who have been taught the game they were to play. You can see All-the-Tiger-there-was smiling at All-the-Bones-there-were, and you can see All-the-Elk-there-was, and All-the-Parrot-there-was, and All-the-Bunnies-there-were on the hill. The other Animals are on the other side of the hill, so I haven't drawn them. The little house up the hill is All-the-House-there-was. The Eldest Magician made it to show the Man how to make houses when he wanted to. The Snake round that spiky hill is All-the-Snake-there-was, and he is talking to All-the-Monkey-there-was, and the Monkey is being rude to the Snake, and the Snake is being rude to the Monkey. The Man is very busy talking to the Eldest Magician. The Little Girl-Daughter is looking at Pau Amma as he runs away. That humpy thing in the water in front is Pau Amma. He wasn't a common Crab in those days. He was a King Crab. That is why he looks different. The thing that looks like bricks that the Man is standing in, is the Big Miz-Maze. When the Man has done talking with the Eldest Magician he will walk in the Big Miz-Maze, because he has to. The mark on the stone under the Man's foot is a magic mark; and down underneath I have drawn the three Magic Flowers all mixed up with the Magic Cloud. All this picture is Big Medicine and Strong Magic.

Then the Eldest Magician stood up and shouted, 'Ho! beasts, birds, and fishes, that I took between my hands at the Very Beginning and taught the play that you should play, which one of you is playing with the Sea?'

Then all the beasts, birds, and fishes said together, 'Eldest Magician, we play the plays that you taught us to play – we and our children's children. But not one of us plays with the Sea.'

Then the Moon rose big and full over the water, and the Eldest Magician said to the hunchbacked old man who sits in the Moon spinning a fishing-line with which he hopes one day to catch the World, 'Ho! Fisher of the Moon, are you playing with the Sea?'

'No,' said the Fisherman, 'I am spinning a line with which I shall some day catch the World; but I do not play with the Sea.' And he went on spinning his line.

Now there is also a Rat up in the Moon who always bites the old Fisherman's line as fast as it is made, and the Eldest Magician said to him, 'Ho! Rat of the Moon, are *you* playing with the Sea?'

And the Rat said, 'I am too busy biting through the line that this old Fisherman is spinning. I do not play with the Sea.' And he went on biting the line.

Then the little girl-daughter put up her little soft brown arms with the beautiful white shell bracelets and said, 'O Eldest Magician! when my father here talked to you at the Very Beginning, and I leaned upon his shoulder while the beasts were being taught their plays, one beast went away naughtily into the Sea before you had taught him his play.'

And the Eldest Magician said, 'How wise are little children who see and are silent! What was that beast like?'

And the little girl-daughter said, 'He was round and he was flat; and his eyes grew upon stalks; and he walked sideways like this; and he was covered with strong armour upon his back.'

And the Eldest Magician said, 'How wise are little children who speak truth! Now I know where Pau Amma went. Give me the paddle!'

So he took the paddle; but there was no need to paddle, for

the water flowed steadily past all the islands till they came to the place called Pusat Tasek – the Heart of the Sea – where the great hollow is that leads down to the heart of the world, and in that hollow grows the Wonderful Tree, Pauh Janggi, that bears the magic twin-nuts. Then the Eldest Magician slid his arm up to the shoulder through the deep warm water, and under the roots of the Wonderful Tree he touched the broad back of Pau Amma the Crab. And Pau Amma settled down at the touch, and all the Sea rose up as water rises in a basin when you put your hand into it.

'Ah!' said the Eldest Magician. 'Now I know who has been playing with the Sea'; and he called out, 'What are you doing, Pau Amma?'

And Pau Amma, deep down below, answered, 'Once a day and once a night I go out to look for my food. Once a day and once a night I return. Leave me alone.'

Then the Eldest Magician said, 'Listen, Pau Amma. When you go out from your cave the waters of the Sea pour down into Pusat Tasek, and all the beaches of all the islands are left bare, and the little fish die, and Raja Moyang Kaban, the King of the Elephants, his legs are made muddy. When you come back and sit in Pusat Tasek, the waters of the Sea rise, and half the little islands are drowned, and the Man's house is flooded, and Raja Abdullah, the King of the Crocodiles, his mouth is filled with the salt water.'

Then Pau Amma, deep down below, laughed and said, 'I did not know I was so important. Henceforward I will go out seven times a day, and the waters shall never be still.'

And the Eldest Magician said, 'I cannot make you play the play you were meant to play, Pau Amma, because you escaped me at the Very Beginning; but if you are not afraid, come up and we will talk about it.'

'I am not afraid,' said Pau Amma, and he rose to the top of the sea in the moonlight. There was nobody in the world so big as Pau Amma – for he was the King Crab of all Crabs. Not a common Crab, but a King Crab. One side of his great shell touched the beach at Sarawak; the other touched the beach at Pahang;[4] and he was taller than the smoke of three volcanoes!

This is the picture of Pau Amma the Crab rising out of the sea as tall as the smoke of three volcanoes. I haven't drawn the three volcanoes, because Pau Amma was so big. Pau Amma is trying to make a Magic, but he is only a silly old King Crab, and so he can't do anything. You can see he is all legs and claws and empty hollow shell. The canoe is the canoe that the Man and the Girl-Daughter and the Eldest Magician sailed from the Perak River in. The Sea is all black and bobbly, because Pau Amma has just risen up out of Pusat Tasek. Pusat Tasek is underneath, so I haven't drawn it. The Man is waving his curvy *kris*-knife at Pau Amma. The Little Girl-Daughter is sitting quietly in the middle of the canoe. She knows she is quite safe with her Daddy. The Eldest Magician is standing up at the other end of the canoe beginning to make a Magic. He has left his magic throne on the beach, and he has taken off his clothes so as not to get wet, and he has left the Magic Cloud behind too, so as not to tip the boat over. The thing that looks like another little canoe outside the real canoe is called an outrigger. It is a piece of wood tied to sticks, and it prevents the canoe from being tipped over. The canoe is made out of one piece of wood, and there is a paddle at one end of it.

As he rose up through the branches of the Wonderful Tree he tore off one of the great twin-fruits – the magic double-kernelled nuts that make people young, – and the little girl-daughter saw it bobbing alongside the canoe, and pulled it in and began to pick out the soft eyes of it with her little golden scissors.

'Now,' said the Magician, 'make a Magic, Pau Amma, to show that you are really important.'

Pau Amma rolled his eyes and waved his legs, but he could only stir up the Sea, because, though he was a King Crab, he was nothing more than a Crab, and the Eldest Magician laughed.

'You are not so important after all, Pau Amma,' he said. 'Now, let *me* try,' and he made a Magic with his left hand – with just the little finger of his left hand – and – lo and behold, Best Beloved, Pau Amma's hard, blue-green-black shell fell off him as a husk falls off a coconut, and Pau Amma was left all soft – soft as the little crabs that you sometimes find on the beach, Best Beloved.

'Indeed, you are very important,' said the Eldest Magician. 'Shall I ask the Man here to cut you with his *kris*? Shall I send for Rajah Moyang Kaban, the King of the Elephants, to pierce you with his tusks? or shall I call Rajah Abdullah, the King of the Crocodiles, to bite you?'

And Pau Amma said, 'I am ashamed! Give me back my hard shell and let me got back to Pusat Tasek, and I will only stir out once a day and once a night to get my food.'

And the Eldest Magician said, 'No, Pau Amma, I will *not* give you back your shell, for you will grow bigger and prouder and stronger, and perhaps you will forget your promise, and you will play with the Sea once more.'

Then Pau Amma said, 'What shall I do? I am so big that I can only hide in Pusat Tasek, and if I go anywhere else, all soft as I am now, the sharks and the dogfish will eat me. And if I go to Pusat Tasek, all soft as I am now, though I may be safe, I can never stir out to get my food, and so I shall die.' Then he waved his legs and lamented.

'Listen, Pau Amma,' said the Eldest Magician. 'I cannot

make you play the play you were meant to play, because you escaped me at the Very Beginning; but if you choose, I can make every stone and every hole and every bunch of weed in all the seas a safe Pusat Tasek for you and your children for always.'

Then Pau Amma said, 'That is good, but I do not choose yet. Look! there is that Man who talked to you at the Very Beginning. If he had not taken up your attention I should not have grown tired of waiting and run away, and all this would never have happened. What will *he* do for me?'

And the Man said, 'If you choose, I will make a Magic, so that both the deep water and the dry ground will be a home for you and your children – so that you shall be able to hide both on the land and in the sea.'

And Pau Amma said, 'I do not choose yet. Look! there is that girl who saw me running away at the Very Beginning. If she had spoken then, the Eldest Magician would have called me back, and all this would never have happened. What will *she* do for me?'

And the little girl-daughter said, 'This is a good nut that I am eating. If you choose, I will make a Magic and I will give you this pair of scissors, very sharp and strong, so that you and your children can eat coconuts like this all day long when you come up from the Sea to the land; or you can dig a Pusat Tasek for yourself with the scissors that belong to you when there is no stone or hole near by; and when the earth is too hard, by the help of these same scissors you can run up a tree.'

And Pau Amma said, 'I do not choose yet, for, all soft as I am, these gifts would not help me. Give me back my shell, O Eldest Magician, and then I will play your play.'

And the Eldest Magician said, 'I will give it back, Pau Amma, for eleven months of the year; but on the twelfth month of every year it shall grow soft again, to remind you and all your children that I can make Magics, and to keep you humble, Pau Amma; for I see that if you can run both under the water and on land, you will grow too bold; and if you can climb trees and crack nuts and dig holes with your scissors, you will grow too greedy, Pau Amma.'

Then Pau Amma thought a little and said, 'I have made my choice. I will take all the gifts.'

Then the Eldest Magician made a Magic with the right hand, with all five fingers of his right hand, and lo and behold, Best Beloved, Pau Amma grew smaller and smaller and smaller, till at last there was only a little green crab swimming in the water alongside the canoe, crying in a very small voice, 'Give me the scissors!'

And the girl-daughter picked him up on the palm of her little brown hand, and sat him on the bottom of the canoe and gave him her scissors, and he waved them in his little arms, and opened them and shut them and snapped them, and said, 'I can eat nuts. I can crack shells. I can dig holes. I can climb trees. I can breathe in the dry air, and I can find a safe Pusat Tasek under every stone. I did not know I was so important. *Kun?*' Is this right?

'*Payah kun*,' said the Eldest Magician, and he laughed and gave him his blessing; and little Pau Amma scuttled over the side of the canoe into the water; and he was so tiny that he could have hidden under the shadow of a dry leaf on land or of a dead shell at the bottom of the sea.

'Was that well done?' said the Eldest Magician.

'Yes,' said the Man. 'But now we must go back to Perak, and that is a weary way to paddle. If we had waited till Pau Amma had gone out of Pusat Tasek and come home, the water would have carried us there by itself.'

'You are lazy,' said the Eldest Magician. 'So your children shall be lazy. They shall be the laziest people in the world. They shall be called the Malazy – the lazy people'; and he held up his finger to the Moon and said, 'O Fisherman, here is this Man too lazy to row home. Pull his canoe home with your line, Fisherman.'

'No,' said the Man. 'If I am to be lazy all my days, let the Sea work for me twice a day for ever. That will save paddling.'

And the Eldest Magician laughed and said, '*Payah kun*' (That is right).

And the Rat of the Moon stopped biting the line; and the Fisherman let his line down till it touched the Sea, and he pulled the whole deep Sea along, past the Island of Bintang, past Singapore, past Malacca, past Selangor, till the canoe whirled into the mouth of the Perak River again.

'*Kun?*' said the Fisherman of the Moon.

'*Payah kun,*' said the Eldest Magician. 'See now that you pull the Sea twice a day and twice a night for ever, so that the Malazy fishermen may be saved paddling. But be careful not to do it too hard, or I shall make a Magic on you as I did to Pau Amma.'

Then they all went up the Perak River and went to bed, Best Beloved.

Now listen and attend!

From that day to this the Moon has always pulled the Sea up and down and made what we call the tides. Sometimes the Fisher of the Sea pulls a little too hard, and then we get spring-tides; and sometimes he pulls a little too softly, and then we get what are called neap-tides; but nearly always he is careful, because of the Eldest Magician.

And Pau Amma? You can see when you go to the beach, how all Pau Amma's babies make little Pusat Taseks for themselves under every stone and bunch of weed on the sands; you can see them waving their little scissors; and in some parts of the world they truly live on the dry land and run up the palm-trees and eat coconuts, exactly as the girl-daughter promised. But once a year all Pau Ammas must shake off their hard armour and be soft – to remind them of what the Eldest Magician could do. And so it isn't fair to kill or hunt Pau Amma's babies just because old Pau Amma was stupidly rude a very long time ago.

Oh yes! And Pau Amma's babies hate being taken out of their little Pusat Taseks and brought home in pickle-bottles. That is why they nip you with their scissors, and it serves you right!

China-going P. and O.'s[5]
Pass Pau Amma's playground close,
And his Pusat Tasek lies
Near the track of most B.I.'s
N.Y.K. and N.D.L.
Know Pau Amma's home as well
As the Fisher of the Sea knows
'Bens,' M.M.'s, and Rubattinos.
But (and this is rather queer)
A.T.L.'s can *not* come here;
O. and O. and D.O.A.
Must go round another way.
Orient, Anchor, Bibby, Hall,
Never go that way at all.
U.C.S. would have a fit
If it found itself on it.
And if 'Beavers' took their cargoes
To Penang instead of Lagos,
Or a fat Shaw-Savill bore
Passengers to Singapore,
Or a White Star were to try a
Little trip to Sourabaya,
Or a B.S.A. went on
Past Natal to Cheribon,
Then great Mr Lloyds would come
With a wire and drag them home!

You'll know what my riddle means
When you've eaten mangosteens.[6]

Or if you can't wait till then, ask them to let you have the
outside page of *The Times*; turn over to page 2, where it is
marked 'Shipping' on the top left hand; then take the Atlas (and
that is the finest picture-book in the world) and see how the
names of the places that the steamers go to fit into the names of
the places on the map. Any steamer-kiddy ought to be able to
do that; but if you can't read, ask some one to show it you.

The Cat that Walked by Himself

EAR and attend and listen; for this befell and be-happened and became and was, O my Best Beloved, when the Tame animals were wild. The Dog was wild, and the Horse was wild, and the Cow was wild, and the Sheep was wild, and the Pig was wild – as wild as wild could be – and they walked in the West Wild Woods by their wild lones. But the wildest of all the wild animals was the Cat. He walked by himself, and all places were alike to him.

Of course the Man was wild too. He was dreadfully wild. He didn't even begin to be tame till he met the Woman, and she told him that she did not like living in his wild ways. She picked out a nice dry Cave, instead of a heap of wet leaves, to lie down in; and she strewed clean sand on the floor; and she lit a nice fire of wood at the back of the Cave; and she hung a dried wild-horse skin, tail-down, across the opening of the Cave; and she said, 'Wipe your feet, dear, when you come in, and now we'll keep house.'

That night, Best Beloved, they ate wild sheep roasted on the hot stones, and flavoured with wild garlic and wild pepper; and wild duck stuffed with wild rice and wild fenugreek[1] and wild coriander; and marrow-bones of wild oxen; and wild cherries, and wild grenadillas.[2] Then the Man went to sleep in front of the fire ever so happy; but the Woman sat up, combing her hair. She took the bone of the shoulder of mutton – the big flat blade-bone – and she looked at the wonderful marks on it, and she threw more wood on the fire, and she made a Magic. She made the First Singing Magic in the world.

Out in the Wet Wild Woods all the wild animals gathered together where they could see the light of the fire a long way off, and they wondered what it meant.

Then Wild Horse stamped with his wild foot and said, 'O my Friends and O my Enemies, why have the Man and the Woman made that great light in that great Cave, and what harm will it do us?'

Wild Dog lifted up his wild nose and smelled the smell of the roast mutton, and said, 'I will go up and see and look, and say; for I think it is good. Cat, come with me.'

'Nenni!'[3] said the Cat. 'I am the Cat who walks by himself, and all places are alike to me. I will not come.'

'Then we can never be friends again,' said Wild Dog, and he trotted off to the Cave. But when he had gone a little way the Cat said to himself, 'All places are alike to me. Why should I not go too and see and look and come away at my own liking?' So he slipped after Wild Dog softly, very softly, and hid himself where he could hear everything.

When Wild Dog reached the mouth of the Cave he lifted up the dried horse-skin with his nose and sniffed the beautiful smell of the roast mutton, and the Woman, looking at the blade-bone, heard him, and laughed, and said, 'Here comes the first. Wild Thing out of the Wild Woods, what do you want?'

Wild Dog said, 'O my Enemy and Wife of my Enemy, what is this that smells so good in the Wild Woods?'

Then the Woman picked up a roasted mutton-bone and threw it to Wild Dog, and said, 'Wild Thing out of the Wild Woods, taste and try.' Wild dog gnawed the bone, and it was more delicious than anything he had ever tasted, and he said, 'O my Enemy and Wife of my Enemy, give me another.'

The Woman said, 'Wild Thing out of the Wild Woods, help my Man to hunt through the day and guard this Cave at night, and I will give you as many roast bones as you need.'

'Ah!' said the Cat, listening. 'This is a very wise Woman, but she is not so wise as I am.'

The Cat that Walked by Himself

Wild Dog crawled into the Cave and laid his head on the Woman's lap, and said, 'O my Friend and Wife of my Friend, I will help your Man to hunt through the day, and at night I will guard your Cave.'

'Ah!' said the Cat, listening. 'That is a very foolish Dog.' And he went back through the Wet Wild Woods waving his wild tail, and walking by his wild lone. But he never told anybody.

When the Man waked up he said, 'What is Wild Dog doing here?' And the Woman said, 'His name is not Wild Dog any more, but the First Friend, because he will be our friend for always and always and always. Take him with you when you go hunting.'

Next night the Woman cut great green armfuls of fresh grass from the water-meadows, and dried it before the fire, so that it smelt like new-mown hay, and she sat at the mouth of the Cave and plaited a halter out of the horse-hide, and she looked at the shoulder-of-mutton bone – at the big broad blade-bone – and she made a Magic. She made the Second Singing Magic in the world.

Out in the Wild Woods all the wild animals wondered what had happened to Wild Dog, and at last Wild Horse stamped his foot and said, 'I will go and see and say why Wild Dog has not returned. Cat, come with me.'

'Nenni!' said the Cat. 'I am the Cat who walks by himself, and all places are alike to me. I will not come.' But all the same he followed Wild Horse softly, very softly, and hid himself where he could hear everything.

When the Woman heard Wild Horse tripping and stumbling on his long mane, she laughed and said, 'Here comes the second. Wild Thing out of the Wild Woods, what do you want?'

Wild Horse said, 'O my Enemy and Wife of my Enemy, where is Wild Dog?'

The Woman laughed, and picked up the blade-bone and looked at it, and said, 'Wild Thing out of the Wild Woods, you did not come here for Wild Dog, but for the sake of this good grass.'

And Wild Horse, tripping and stumbling on his long mane, said, 'That is true; give it me to eat.'

This is the picture of the Cave where the Man and the Woman lived first of all. It was really a very nice Cave, and much warmer than it looks. The Man had a canoe. It is on the edge of the river, being soaked in water to make it swell up. The tattery-looking thing across the river is the Man's salmon-net to catch salmon with. There are nice clean stones leading up from the river to the mouth of the Cave, so that the Man and the Woman could go down for water without getting sand between their toes. The things like blackbeetles far down the beach are really trunks of dead trees that floated down the river from the Wet Wild Woods on the other bank. The Man and the Woman used to drag them out and dry them and cut them up for firewood. I haven't drawn the horse-hide curtain at the mouth of the Cave, because the Woman has just taken it down to be cleaned. All those little smudges on the sand between Cave and the river are the marks of the Woman's feet and the Man's feet.

The Man and the Woman are both inside the Cave eating their dinner. They went to another cosier Cave when the Baby came, because the Baby used to crawl down to the river and fall in, and the Dog had to pull him out.

The Woman said, 'Wild Thing out of the Wild Woods, bend you wild head and wear what I give you, and you shall eat the wonderful grass three times a day.'

'Ah!' said the Cat, listening. 'This is a clever Woman, but she is not so clever as I am.'

Wild Horse bent his wild head, and the Woman slipped the plaited-hide halter over it, and Wild Horse breathed on the Woman's feet and said, 'O my Mistress, and Wife of my Master, I will be your servant for the sake of the wonderful grass.'

'Ah!' said the Cat, listening. 'That is a very foolish Horse.' And he went back through the Wet Wild Woods, waving his wild tail and walking by his wild lone. But he never told anybody.

When the Man and the Dog came back from hunting, the Man said, 'What is Wild Horse doing here?' And the Woman said, 'His name is not Wild Horse any more, but the First Servant, because he will carry us from place to place for always and always and always. Ride on his back when you go hunting.'

Next day, holding her wild head high that her wild horns should not catch in the wild trees, Wild Cow came up to the Cave, and the Cat followed, and hid himself just the same as before; and everything happened just the same as before; and the Cat said the same things as before; and when Wild Cow had promised to give her milk to the Woman every day in exchange for the wonderful grass, the Cat went back through the Wet Wild Woods waving his wild tail and walking by his wild lone, just the same as before. But he never told anybody. And when the Man and the Horse and the Dog came home from hunting and asked the same questions same as before, the Woman said, 'Her name is not Wild Cow any more, but the Giver of Good Food. She will give us the warm white milk for always and always and always, and I will take care of her while you and the First Friend and the First Servant go hunting.'

Next day the Cat waited to see if any other Wild Thing would go up to the Cave, but no one moved in the Wet Wild Woods, so the Cat walked there by himself; and he saw the Woman milking the Cow, and he saw the light of the fire in the Cave, and he smelt the smell of the warm white milk.

Cat said, 'O my Enemy and Wife of my Enemy, where did Wild Cow go?'

The Woman laughed and said, 'Wild Thing out of the Wild Woods, go back to the Woods again, for I have braided up my hair, and I have put away the magic blade-bone, and we have no more need of either friends or servants in our Cave.'

Cat said, 'I am not a friend, and I am not a servant. I am the Cat who walks by himself, and I wish to come into your Cave.'

Woman said, 'Then why did you not come with First Friend on the first night?'

Cat grew very angry and said, 'Has Wild Dog told tales of me?'

Then the Woman laughed and said, 'You are the Cat who walks by himself, and all places are alike to you. You are neither a friend nor a servant. You have said it yourself. Go away and walk by yourself in all places alike.'

Then Cat pretended to be sorry and said, 'Must I never come into the Cave? Must I never sit by the warm fire? Must I never drink the warm white milk? You are very wise and very beautiful. You should not be cruel even to a Cat.'

Woman said, 'I knew I was wise, but I did not know I was beautiful. So I will make a bargain with you. If ever I say one word in your praise, you may come into the Cave.'

'And if you say two words in my praise?' said the Cat.

'I never shall,' said the Woman, 'but if I say two words in your praise, you may sit by the fire in the Cave.'

'And if you say three words?' said the Cat.

'I never shall,' said the Woman, 'but if I say three words in your praise, you may drink the warm white milk three times a day for always and always and always.'

Then the Cat arched his back and said, 'Now let the Curtain at the mouth of the Cave, and the Fire at the back of the Cave, and the Milk-pots that stand beside the Fire, remember what my Enemy and the Wife of my Enemy has said.' And he went away through the Wet Wild Woods waving his wild tail and walking by his wild lone.

This is the picture of the Cat that Walked by Himself, walking by his wild lone through the Wet Wild Woods and waving his wild tail. There is nothing else in the picture except some toadstools. They had to grow there because the woods were so wet. The lumpy thing on the low branch isn't a bird. It is moss that grew there because the Wild Woods were so wet.

Underneath the truly picture is a picture of the cosy Cave that the Man and the Woman went to after the Baby came. It was their summer Cave, and they planted wheat in front of it. The Man is riding on the Horse to find the Cow and bring her back to the Cave to be milked. He is holding up his hand to call the Dog, who has swum across to the other side of the river, looking for rabbits.

That night when the Man and the Horse and the Dog came home from hunting, the Woman did not tell them of the bargain that she had made with the Cat, because she was afraid that they might not like it.

Cat went far and far away and hid himself in the Wet Wild Woods by his wild lone for a long time till the Woman forgot all about him. Only the Bat – the little upside-down Bat – that hung inside the Cave knew where Cat hid; and every evening Bat would fly to Cat with news of what was happening.

One evening Bat said, 'There is a Baby in the Cave. He is new and pink and fat and small, and the Woman is very fond of him.'

'Ah,' said the Cat, listening. 'But what is the Baby fond of?'

'He is fond of things that are soft and tickle,' said the Bat. 'He is fond of warm things to hold in his arms when he goes to sleep. He is fond of being played with. He is fond of all those things.'

'Ah,' said the Cat, listening. 'Then my time has come.'

Next night Cat walked through the Wet Wild Woods and hid very near the Cave till morning-time, and Man and Dog and Horse went hunting. The Woman was busy cooking that morning, and the Baby cried and interrupted. So she carried him outside the Cave and gave him a handful of pebbles to play with. But still the Baby cried.

Then the Cat put out his paddy paw and patted the Baby on the cheek, and it cooed; and the Cat rubbed against its fat knees and tickled it under its fat chin with his tail. And the Baby laughed; and the Woman heard him and smiled.

Then the Bat – the little upside-down Bat – that hung in the mouth of the Cave said, 'O my Hostess and Wife of my Host and Mother of my Host's Son, a Wild Thing from the Wild Woods is most beautifully playing with your Baby.'

'A blessing on that Wild Thing whoever he may be,' said the Woman, straightening her back, 'for I was a busy woman this morning and he has done me a service.'

That very minute and second, Best Beloved, the dried horse-skin Curtain that was stretched tail-down at the mouth of the Cave fell down – *woosh!* – because it remembered the bargain she had made with the Cat; and when the Woman went to pick it up – lo and behold! – the Cat was sitting quite comfy inside the Cave.

'O my Enemy and Wife of my Enemy and Mother of my Enemy,' said the Cat, 'it is I: for you have spoken a word in my praise, and now I can sit within the Cave for always and always and always. But still I am the Cat who walks by himself, and all places are alike to me.'

The Woman was very angry, and shut her lips tight and took up her spinning-wheel and began to spin.

But the Baby cried because the Cat had gone away, and the Woman could not hush it, for it struggled and kicked and grew black in the face.

'O my Enemy and Wife of my Enemy and Mother of my Enemy,' said the Cat, 'take a strand of the thread that you are spinning and tie it to your spinning-whorl and drag it along the floor, and I will show you a Magic that shall make your Baby laugh as loudly as he is now crying.'

'I will do so,' said the Woman, 'because I am at my wits' end; but I will not thank you for it.'

She tied the thread to the little clay spindle-whorl and drew it across the floor, and the Cat ran after it and patted it with his paws and rolled head over heels, and tossed it backward over his shoulder and chased it between his hind legs and pretended to lose it, and pounced down upon it again, till the Baby laughed as loudly as it had been crying, and scrambled after the Cat and frolicked all over the Cave till it grew tired and settled down to sleep with the Cat in its arms.

'Now,' said Cat, 'I will sing the Baby a song that shall keep him asleep for an hour.' And he began to purr, loud and low, low and loud, till the Baby fell fast asleep. The Woman smiled as she looked down upon the two of them, and said, 'That was wonderfully done. No question but you are very clever, O Cat.'

That very minute and second, Best Beloved, the smoke of the Fire at the back of the Cave came down in clouds from the roof – *puff!* – because it remembered the bargain she had made with the Cat; and when it had cleared away – lo and behold! – the Cat was sitting quite comfy close to the fire.

'O my Enemy and Wife of my Enemy and Mother of my Enemy,' said the Cat, 'it is I: for you have spoken a second word in my praise, and now I can sit by the warm fire at the back of the Cave for always and always and always. But still I am the Cat who walks by himself, and all places are alike to me.'

Then the Woman was very very angry, and let down her hair and put more wood on the fire and brought out the broad blade-bone of the shoulder of mutton and began to make a Magic that should prevent her from saying a third word in praise of the Cat. It was not a Singing Magic, Best Beloved, it was a Still Magic; and by and by the Cave grew so still that a little wee-wee mouse crept out of a corner and ran across the floor.

'O my Enemy and Wife of my Enemy and Mother of my Enemy,' said the Cat, 'is that little mouse part of your Magic?'

'Ouh! Chee! No indeed!' said the Woman, and she dropped the blade-bone and jumped upon the footstool in front of the fire and braided up her hair very quick for fear that the mouse should run up it.

'Ah,' said the Cat, watching. 'Then the mouse will do me no harm if I eat it?'

'No,' said the Woman, braiding up her hair, 'eat it quickly and I will ever be grateful to you.'

Cat made one jump and caught the little mouse, and the Woman said, 'A hundred thanks. Even the First Friend is not quick enough to catch little mice as you have done. You must be very wise.'

That very moment and second, O Best Beloved, the Milk-pot that stood by the fire cracked in two pieces – *ffft!* – because it remembered the bargain she had made with the Cat; and when the Woman jumped down from the footstool – lo and behold! – the Cat was lapping up the warm white milk that lay in one of the broken pieces.

'O my Enemy and Wife of my Enemy and Mother of my Enemy,' said the Cat, 'it is I: for you have spoken three words in my praise, and now I can drink the warm white milk three times a day for always and always and always. But *still* I am the Cat who walks by himself, and all places are alike to me.'

The Cat that Walked by Himself

Then the Woman laughed and set the Cat a bowl of the warm white milk and said, 'O Cat, you are as clever as a man, but remember that your bargain was not made with the Man or the Dog, and I do not know what they will do when they come home.'

'What is that to me?' said the Cat. 'If I have my place in the Cave by the fire and my warm white milk three times a day I do not care what the Man or the Dog can do.'

That evening when the Man and the Dog came into the Cave, the Woman told them all the story of the bargain, while the Cat sat by the fire and smiled. Then the Man said, 'Yes, but he has not made a bargain with *me* or with all proper Men after me.' Then he took off his two leather boots and he took up his little stone axe (that makes three) and he fetched a piece of wood and a hatchet (that is five altogether), and he set them out in a row and he said, 'Now we will make *our* bargain. If you do not catch mice when you are in the Cave for always and always and always, I will throw these five things at you whenever I see you, and so shall all proper Men do after me.'

'Ah!' said the Woman, listening. 'This is a very clever Cat, but he is not so clever as my Man.'

The Cat counted the five things (and they looked very knobby) and he said, 'I will catch mice when I am in the Cave for always and always and always; but *still* I am the Cat who walks by himself, and all places are alike to me.'

'Not when I am near,' said the Man. 'If you had not said that last I would have put all these things away for always and always and always; but now I am going to throw my two boots and my little stone axe (that makes three) at you whenever I meet you. And so shall all proper Men do after me!'

Then the Dog said, 'Wait a minute. He has not made a bargain with *me* or with all proper Dogs after me.' And he showed his teeth and said, 'If you are not kind to the Baby while I am in the Cave for always and always an always, I will hunt you till I catch you, and when I catch you I will bite you. And so shall all proper Dogs do after me.'

'Ah!' said the Woman, listening. 'This is a very clever Cat, but he is not so clever as the Dog.'

Cat counted the Dog's teeth (and they looked very pointed) and he said, 'I will be kind to the Baby while I am in the Cave, as long as he does not pull my tail too hard, for always and always and always. But *still* I am the Cat that walks by himself, and all places are alike to me.'

'Not when I am near,' said the Dog. 'If you had not said that last I would have shut my mouth for always and always and always; but *now* I am going to hunt you up a tree whenever I meet you. And so shall all proper Dogs do after me.'

Then the Man threw his two boots and his little stone axe (that makes three) at the Cat, and the Cat ran out of the Cave and the Dog chased him up a tree; and from that day to this, Best Beloved, three proper Men out of five will always throw things at a Cat whenever they meet him, and all proper Dogs will chase him up a tree. But the Cat keeps his side of the bargain too. He will kill mice, and he will be kind to Babies when he is in the house, just as long as they do not pull his tail too hard. But when he has done that, and between times, and when the moon gets up and night comes, he is the Cat that walks by himself, and all places are alike to him. Then he goes out to the Wet Wild Woods or up the Wet Wild Trees or on the Wet Wild Roofs, waving his wild tail and walking by his wild lone.

Pussy can sit by the fire and sing,
    Pussy can climb a tree,
Or play with a silly old cork and string
    To 'muse herself, not me.
But I like *Binkie* my dog, because
    He knows how to behave;
So, *Binkie's* the same as the First Friend was,
    And I am the Man in the Cave!

Pussy will play man-Friday till
    It's time to wet her paw
And make her walk on the window-sill
    (For the footprint Crusoe saw);
Then she fluffles her tail and mews,
    And scratches and won't attend.
But *Binkie* will play whatever I choose,
    And he is my true First Friend!

Pussy will rub my knees with her head
    Pretending she loves me hard;
But the very minute I go to my bed
    Pussy runs out in the yard,
And there she stays till the morning-light;
    So I know it is only pretend;
But *Binkie*, he snores at my feet all night,
    And he is my Firstest Friend!

The Butterfly that Stamped

HIS, O my Best Beloved, is a story – a story quite different from the other stories – a story about The Most Wise Sovereign Suleiman-bin-Daoud – Solomon the Son of David.

There are three hundred and fifty-five stories about Suleiman-bin-Daoud; but this is not one of them. It is not the story of the Lapwing who found the Water;[1] or the Hoopoe[2] who shaded Suleiman-bin-Daoud from the heat. It is not the story of the Glass Pavement, or the Ruby with the Crooked Hole, or the Gold Bars of Balkis. It is the story of the Butterfly that Stamped.

Now attend all over again and listen!

Suleiman-bin-Daoud was wise. He understood what the beasts said, what the birds said, what the fishes said, and what the insects said. He understood what the rocks said deep under the earth when they bowed in towards each other and groaned; and he understood what the trees said when they rustled in the middle of the morning. He understood everything, from the bishop on the bench to the hyssop[3] on the wall; and Balkis, his Head Queen, the Most Beautiful Queen Balkis, was nearly as wise as he was.

Suleiman-bin-Daoud was strong. Upon the third finger of his right hand he wore a ring. When he turned it once, Afrits and Djinns came out of the earth to do whatever he told them. When he turned it twice, Fairies came down from the sky to do whatever he told them; and when he turned it three times, the very great angel Azrael of the Sword came dressed as a water-carrier, and told him the news of the three worlds, – Above – Below – and Here.

And yet Suleiman-bin-Daoud was not proud. He very seldom showed off, and when he did he was sorry for it. Once he tried to feed all the animals in all the world in one day, but when the food was ready an Animal came out of the deep sea and ate it up in three mouthfuls. Suleiman-bin-Daoud was very surprised and said, 'O Animal, who are you?' And the Animal said, 'O King, live for ever! I am the smallest of thirty thousand brothers, and our home is at the bottom of the sea. We heard that you were going to feed all the animals in all the world, and my brothers sent me to ask when dinner would be ready.' Suleiman-bin-Daoud was more surprised than ever and said, 'O Animal, you have eaten all the dinner that I made ready for all the animals in the world.' And the Animal said, 'O King, live for ever, but do you really call *that* a dinner? Where I come from we each eat twice as much as that between meals.' Then Suleiman-bin-Daoud fell flat on his face and said, 'O Animal! I gave that dinner to show what a great and rich king I was, and not because I really wanted to be kind to the animals. Now I am ashamed, and it serves me right.' Suleiman-bin-Daoud was a really truly wise man, Best Beloved. After that he never forgot that it was silly to show off; and now the real story part of my story begins.

He married ever so many wives. He married nine hundred and ninety-nine wives, besides the Most Beautiful Balkis; and they all lived in a great golden palace in the middle of a lovely garden with fountains. He didn't really want nine hundred and ninety-nine wives, but in those days everybody married ever so many wives, and of course the King had to marry ever so many more just to show that he was the King.

Some of the wives were nice, but some were simply horrid, and the horrid ones quarrelled with the nice ones and made them horrid too, and then they would all quarrel with Suleiman-bin-Daoud, and that was horrid for him. But Balkis the Most Beautiful never quarrelled with Suleiman-bin-Daoud. She loved him too much. She sat in her rooms in the

This is the picture of the Animal that came out of the sea and ate up all the food that Suleiman-bin-Daoud had made ready for all the animals in all the world. He was really quite a nice Animal, and his Mummy was very fond of him and of his twenty-nine thousand nine hundred and ninety-nine other brothers that lived at the bottom of the sea. You know that he was the smallest of them all, and so his name was Small Porgies. He ate up all those boxes and packets and bales and things that had been got ready for all the animals, without ever once taking off the lids or untying the strings, and it did not hurt him at all. The sticky-up masts behind the boxes of food belong to Suleiman-bin-Daoud's ships. They were busy bringing more food when Small Porgies came ashore. He did not eat the ships. They stopped unloading the foods and instantly sailed away to sea till Small Porgies had quite finished eating. You can see some of the ships beginning to sail away by Small Porgies' shoulder. I have not drawn Suleiman-bin-Daoud, but he is just outside the picture, very much astonished. The bundle hanging from the mast of the ship in the corner is really a package of wet dates for parrots to eat. I don't know the names of the ships. That is all there is in that picture.

Golden Palace, or walked in the Palace garden, and was truly sorry for him.

Of course if he had chosen to turn his ring on his finger and call up the Djinns and the Afrits they would have magicked all those nine hundred and ninety-nine quarrelsome wives into white mules of the desert or greyhounds or pomegranate seeds; but Suleiman-bin-Daoud thought that that would be showing off. So, when they quarrelled too much, he only walked by himself in one part of the beautiful Palace gardens and wished he had never been born.

One day, when they had quarrelled for three weeks – all nine hundred and ninety-nine wives together – Suleiman-bin-Daoud went out for peace and quiet as usual; and among the orange-trees he met Balkis the Most Beautiful, very sorrowful because Suleiman-bin-Daoud was so worried. And she said to him, 'O my Lord and Light of my Eyes, turn the ring upon your finger and show these Queens of Egypt and Mesopotamia and Persia and China that you are the great and terrible King.' But Suleiman-bin-Daoud shook his head and said, 'O my Lady and Delight of my Life, remember the Animal that came out of the sea and made me ashamed before all the animals in all the world because I showed off. Now, if I showed off before these Queens of Persia and Egypt and Abyssinia and China, merely because they worry me, I might be made even more ashamed than I have been.'

And Balkis the Most Beautiful said, 'O my Lord and Treasure of my Soul, what will you do?'

And Suleiman-bin-Daoud said, 'O my Lady and Content of my Heart, I shall continue to endure my fate at the hands of these nine hundred and ninety-nine Queens who vex me with their continual quarrelling.'

So he went on between the lilies and the loquats and the roses and the cannas and the heavy-scented ginger-plants that grew in the garden, till he came to the great camphor-tree that was called the Camphor-Tree of Suleiman-bin-Daoud. But Balkis hid among the tall irises and the spotted bamboos and the red lilies behind the camphor-tree, so as to be near her own true love, Suleiman-bin-Daoud.

Presently two Butterflies flew under the tree, quarrelling.

Suleiman-bin-Daoud heard one say to the other, 'I wonder at your presumption in talking like this to me. Don't you know that if I stamped my foot all Suleiman-bin-Daoud's Palace and this garden here would immediately vanish in a clap of thunder?'

Then Suleiman-bin-Daoud forgot his nine hundred and ninety-nine bothersome wives, and laughed, till the camphor-tree shook, at the Butterfly's boast. And he held out his finger and said, 'Little man, come here.'

The Butterfly was dreadfully frightened, but he managed to fly up to the hand of Suleiman-bin-Daoud, and clung there, fanning himself. Suleiman-bin-Daoud bent his head and whispered very softly, 'Little man, you know that all your stamping wouldn't bend one blade of grass. What made you tell that awful fib to your wife? – for doubtless she is your wife.'

The Butterfly looked at Suleiman-bin-Daoud and saw the most wise King's eyes twinkle like stars on a frosty night, and he picked up his courage with both wings, and he put his head on one side and said, 'O King, live for ever! She *is* my wife; and you know what wives are like.'

Suleiman-bin-Daoud smiled in his beard and said, 'Yes, *I* know, little brother.'

'One must keep them in order somehow,' said the Butterfly, 'and she has been quarrelling with me all the morning. I said that to quiet her.'

And Suleiman-bin-Daoud said, 'May it quiet her. Go back to your wife, little brother, and let me hear what you say.'

Back flew the Butterfly to his wife, who was all of a twitter behind a leaf, and she said, 'He heard you! Suleiman-bin-Daoud himself heard you!'

'Heard me!' said the Butterfly. 'Of course he did. I meant him to hear me.'

'And what did he say? Oh, what did he say?'

'Well,' said the Butterfly, fanning himself most importantly, 'between you and me, my dear – of course I don't blame him, because his Palace must have cost a great deal and the oranges are just ripening, – he asked me not to stamp, and I promised I wouldn't.'

'Gracious!' said his wife, and sat quite quiet; but Suleiman-bin-Daoud laughed till the tears ran down his face at the impudence of the bad little Butterfly.

Balkis the Most Beautiful stood up behind the tree among the red lilies and smiled to herself, for she had heard all this talk. She thought, 'If I am wise I can yet save my Lord from the persecutions of these quarrelsome Queens,' and she held out her finger and whispered softly to the Butterfly's Wife, 'Little woman, come here.' Up flew the Butterfly's Wife, very frightened, and clung to Balkis's white hand.

Balkis bent her beautiful head down and whispered, 'Little woman, do you believe what your husband has just said?'

The Butterfly's Wife looked at Balkis, and saw the Most Beautiful Queen's eyes shining like deep pools with starlight on them, and she picked up her courage with both wings and said, 'O Queen, be lovely for ever. *You* know what men-folk are like.'

And the Queen Balkis, the Wise Balkis of Sheba, put her hand to her lips to hide a smile and said, 'Little sister, *I* know.'

'They get angry,' said the Butterfly's Wife, fanning herself quickly, 'over nothing at all, but we must humour them, O Queen. They never mean half they say. If it pleases my husband to believe that I believe he can make Suleiman-bin-Daoud's Palace disappear by stamping his foot, I'm sure *I* don't care. He'll forget all about it tomorrow.'

'Little sister,' said Balkis, 'you are quite right; but next time he begins to boast, take him at his word. Ask him to stamp, and see what will happen. *We* know what men-folk are like, don't we? He'll be very much ashamed.'

Away flew the Butterfly's Wife to her husband, and in five minutes they were quarrelling worse than ever.

'Remember!' said the Butterfly. 'Remember what I can do if I stamp my foot.'

'I don't believe you one little bit,' said the Butterfly's Wife. 'I should very much like to see it done. Suppose you stamp now.'

The Butterfly that Stamped

'I promised Suleiman-bin-Daoud that I wouldn't,' said the Butterfly, 'and I don't want to break my promise.'

'It wouldn't matter if you did,' said his wife. 'You couldn't bend a blade of grass with your stamping. I dare you to do it,' she said. 'Stamp! Stamp! Stamp!'

Suleiman-bin-Daoud, sitting under the camphor-tree, heard every word of this, and he laughed as he had never laughed in his life before. He forgot all about his Queens; he forgot about the Animal that came out of the sea; he forgot about showing off. He just laughed with joy, and Balkis, on the other side of the tree, smiled because her own true love was so joyful.

Presently the Butterfly, very hot and puffy, came whirling back under the shadow of the camphor-tree and said to Suleiman, 'She wants me to stamp! She wants to see what will happen, O Suleiman-bin-Daoud! You know I can't do it, and now she'll never believe a word I say. She'll laugh at me to the end of my days!'

'No, little brother,' said Suleiman-bin-Daoud, 'she will never laugh at you again,' and he turned the ring on his finger – just for the little Butterfly's sake, not for the sake of showing off, – and, lo and behold, four huge Djinns came out of the earth!

'Slaves,' said Suleiman-bin-Daoud, 'when this gentleman on my finger' (that was where the impudent Butterfly was sitting) 'stamps his left front forefoot you will make my Palace and these gardens disappear in a clap of thunder. When he stamps again you will bring them back carefully.'

'Now, little brother,' he said, 'go back to your wife and stamp all you've a mind to.'

Away flew the Butterfly to his wife, who was crying, 'I dare you to do it! I dare you to do it! Stamp! Stamp now! Stamp!' Balkis saw the four vast Djinns stoop down to the four corners of the gardens with the Palace in the middle, and she clapped her hands softly and said, 'At last Suleiman-bin-Daoud will do for the sake of a Butterfly what he ought to have done long ago for his own sake, and the quarrelsome Queens will be frightened!'

Then the Butterfly stamped. The Djinns jerked the Palace and the gardens a thousand miles into the air: there was a most awful thunder-clap, and everything grew inky black. The Butterfly's Wife fluttered about in the dark, crying, 'Oh, I'll be good! I'm so sorry I spoke! Only bring the gardens back, my dear darling husband, and I'll never contradict again.'

The Butterfly was nearly as frightened as his wife, and Suleiman-bin-Daoud laughed so much that it was several minutes before he found breath enough to whisper to the Butterfly, 'Stamp again, little brother. Give me back my Palace, most great magician.'

'Yes, give him back his Palace,' said the Butterfly's Wife, still flying about in the dark like a moth. 'Give him back his Palace, and don't let's have any more horrid magic.'

'Well, my dear,' said the Butterfly as bravely as he could, 'you see what your nagging has led to. Of course it doesn't make any difference to *me* – I'm used to this kind of thing – but as a favour to you and to Suleiman-bin-Daoud I don't mind putting things right.'

So he stamped once more, and that instant the Djinns let down the Palace and the gardens, without even a bump. The sun shone on the dark-green orange-leaves; the fountains played among the pink Egyptian lilies; the birds went on singing; and the Butterfly's Wife lay on her side under the camphor-tree waggling her wings and panting, 'Oh, I'll be good! I'll be good!'

Suleiman-bin-Daoud could hardly speak for laughing. He leaned back all weak and hiccoughy, and shook his finger at the Butterfly and said, 'O great wizard, what is the sense of returning to me my Palace if at the same time you slay me with mirth?'

Then came a terrible noise, for all the nine hundred and ninety-nine Queens ran out of the Palace shrieking and shouting and calling for their babies. They hurried down the great marble steps below the fountain, one hundred abreast, and the Most Wise Balkis went statelily forward to meet them and said, 'What is your trouble, O Queens?'

They stood on the marble steps one hundred abreast and

shouted, '*What* is our trouble? We are living peacefully in our golden Palace, as is our custom, when upon a sudden the Palace disappeared, and we were left sitting in a thick and noisome darkness; and it thundered, and Djinns and Afrits moved about in the darkness! *That* is our trouble, O Head Queen, and we are most extremely troubled on account of that trouble, for it was a troublesome trouble, unlike any trouble we have known.'

Then Balkis the Most Beautiful Queen – Suleiman-bin-Daoud's Very Best Beloved – Queen that was of Sheba and Sabie and the Rivers of the Gold of the South – from the Desert of Zinn to the Towers of Zimbabwe – Balkis, almost as wise as the Most Wise Suleiman-bin-Daoud himself, said, 'It is nothing, O Queens! A Butterfly has made complaint against his wife because she quarrelled with him, and it has pleased our Lord Suleiman-bin-Daoud to teach her a lesson in low-speaking and humbleness, for that is counted a virtue among the wives of the butterflies.'

Then up and spoke an Egyptian Queen – the daughter of a Pharaoh – and she said, 'Our Palace cannot be plucked up by the roots like a leek for the sake of a little insect. No! Suleiman-bin-Daoud must be dead, and what we heard and saw was the earth thundering and darkening at the news.'

Then Balkis beckoned that bold Queen without looking at her, and said to her and to the others, 'Come and see.'

They came down the marble steps, one hundred abreast, and beneath his camphor-tree, still weak with laughing, they saw the Most Wise King Suleiman-bin-Daoud rocking back and forth with a Butterfly on either hand, and they heard him say, 'O wife of my brother in the air, remember after this to please your husband in all things, lest he be provoked to stamp his foot yet again; for he has said that he is used to this Magic, and he is most eminently a great magician – one who steals away the very Palace of Suleiman-bin-Daoud himself. Go in peace, little folk!' And he kissed them on the wings, and they flew away.

Then all the Queens except Balkis – the Most Beautiful and Splendid Balkis, who stood apart smiling – fell flat on their

This is the picture of the four gull-winged Djinns lifting up Suleiman-bin-Daoud's Palace the very minute after the Butterfly had stamped. The Palace and the gardens and everything came up in one piece like a board, and they left a big hole in the ground all full of dust and smoke. If you look in the corner, close to the thing that looks like a lion, you will see Suleiman-bin-Daoud with his magic stick and the two Butterflies behind him. The thing that looks like a lion is really a lion carved in stone, and the thing that looks like a milk-can is really a piece of a temple or a house or something. Suleiman-bin-Daoud stood there so as to be out of the way of the dust and the smoke when the Djinns lifted up the Palace. I don't know the Djinns' names. They were servants of Suleiman-bin-Daoud's magic ring, and they changed about every day. They were just common gull-winged Djinns.

The thing at the bottom is a picture of a very friendly Djinn called Akraig. He used to feed the little fishes in the sea three times a day, and his wings were made of pure copper. I put him in to show you what a nice Djinn is like. He did not help to lift the Palace. He was busy feeding little fishes in the Arabian Sea when it happened.

faces, for they said, 'If these things are done when a Butterfly is displeased with his wife, what shall be done to us who have vexed our King with our loud-speaking and open quarrelling through many days?'

Then they put their veils over their heads, and they put their hands over their mouths, and they tiptoed back to the Palace most mousy-quiet.

Then Balkis – the Most Beautiful and Excellent Balkis – went forward through the red lilies into the shade of the camphor-tree and laid her hand upon Suleiman-bin-Daoud's shoulder and said, 'O my Lord and Treasure of my Soul, rejoice, for we have taught the Queens of Egypt and Mesopotamia and Abyssinia and Persia and India and China with a great and a memorable teaching.'

And Suleiman-bin-Daoud, still looking after the Butterflies where they played in the sunlight, said, 'O my Lady and Jewel of my Felicity, when did this happen? For I have been jesting with a Butterfly ever since I came into the garden.' And he told Balkis what he had done.

Balkis – the Tender and Most Lovely Balkis – said, 'O my Lord and Regent of my Existence, I hid behind the camphor-tree and saw it all. It was I who told the Butterfly's Wife to ask the Butterfly to stamp, because I hoped that for the sake of the jest my Lord would make some great Magic and that the Queens would see it and be frightened.' And she told him what the Queens had said and seen and thought.

Then Suleiman-bin-Daoud rose up from his seat under the camphor-tree, and stretched his arms and rejoiced and said, 'O my Lady and Sweetener of my Days, know that if I had made a Magic against my Queens for the sake of pride or anger, as I made that feast for all the animals, I should certainly have been put to shame. But by means of your wisdom I made the Magic for the sake of a jest and for the sake of a little Butterfly, and – behold – it has also delivered me from the vexations of my vexatious wives! Tell me, therefore, O my Lady and Heart of my Heart, how did you come to be so wise?'

And Balkis the Queen, beautiful and tall, looked up into Suleiman-bin-Daoud's eyes and put her head a little on one side, just like the Butterfly, and said, 'First, O my Lord, because I loved you; and secondly, O my Lord, because I know what women-folk are.'

Then they went up to the Palace and lived happily ever afterwards.

But wasn't it clever of Balkis?

There was never a Queen like Balkis,
  From here to the wide world's end;
But Balkis talked to a butterfly
  As you would talk to a friend.

There was never a King like Solomon,
  Not since the world began;
But Solomon talked to a butterfly
  As a man would talk to a man.

She was Queen of Sabæa[4] –
  And *he* was Asia's Lord –
But they both of 'em talked to butterflies
  When they took their walks abroad!

THE END

Notes

How the Whale got his Throat

1. *'Stute*: astute, clever.
2. *Cetacean*: genus of the whale.
3. *picture of the Whale*: Kipling describes the genesis of this drawing in his autobiographical *Something of Myself*: 'On one trip our steamer came almost atop of a whale, who submerged just in time to clear us, and looked up into my face with an unforgettable little eye the size of a bullock's . . . When I was illustrating the *Just So Stories*, I remembered and strove after that eye.'
4. *Suspenders*: American term for braces.
5. *jaws-of-a-gaff*: a gaff is a spar. Its jaws clasp the mast while allowing the gaff to swing freely.
6. *A.B.*: able-bodied seaman.
7. *latitude Fifty North, longitude Forty West*: in the North Atlantic.
8. Sloka: verse epigram, boastful or magical.

How the Camel got his Hump

1. *indaba, punchayet*: council.

How the Rhinoceros got his Skin

1. *Parsee*: Persian sun-worshipper. (This is a crude definition, but it is what Kipling means.)
2. *Mazanderan, Socotra, and the Promontories of the Larger Equinox*: respectively a province of Iran, an island in the Indian Ocean and a piece of imaginary geography.
3. *Orotavo, Amygdala, Anantarivo, Sonaput*: imaginary places, but ones that echo the names of real places (e.g. Sonapur in India).
4. *the Pink Arabian Sea*: the Red Sea.

167

How the Leopard got his Spots

1. *the High Veldt*: the steppe-like plateau extending through most of what was Basutoland, the Orange Free State and the Southern Transvaal.
2. *Eland, Koodoo, Hartebeest*: large species of African antelope.
3. *Bush-Buck, Bonte-Buck*: male deer.
4. *Quagga*: a quadruped related to the zebra, now extinct.
5. *fulvous:* yellow.
6. *Coptic*, etc.: *Coptic*: Egyptian; *Hieroglyphic*: Ancient Egyptian; *Cuneiformic*: Cuneiform, Hittite; *Bengalic*: Bengali; *Burmic*: Burmese; *Hebric*: Hebrew.
7. *pudding-stone*: a composite rock of rounded pebbles in a silicious matrix.
8. *'Can the Ethiopian . . . ?'*: Jeremiah xiii. 23.

The Elephant's Child

1. *Precession*: proper order obtained by calculation.
2. *wait-a-bit thorn-bush*: bush indigenous to South Africa, so called because of the deterrent effect of its strong spines.
3. *Limpopo River*: the Limpopo, or Crocodile, in South-East Africa is over 1,000 miles long and, next to the Zambesi, the longest river of Africa entering the Indian Ocean.
4. *Khama's Country*: Khama was chief of the Bamangwato, the largest and most important tribe in Botswanaland.
5. *double-clove-hitch*: a type of knot.
6. *Pachyderm*: a mammal with a thick skin, such as an elephant or a rhinoceros.

The Sing-Song of Old Man Kangaroo

1. *Dingo*: the Australian dingo resembles a fox in appearance.
2. *Boomer*. Australian name for a kangaroo.
3. *spinifex*: spiny Australian grass.
4. *ti-trees*: Polynesian name for certain trees with edible roots.
5. *mulga*: Australian name for bush country.

6. *Wollgong River*: imaginary.
7. *Flinders*: a river, a range of mountains, an island, a reef, a bay and a county, all named after Matthew Flinders (1774–1814), an English naval officer who circumnavigated Australia and charted the Gulf of Carpentaria.
8. *Darling Downs*: a plain in southern Queensland.
9. *played Old Scratch*: played the Devil.

The Beginning of the Armadilloes

1. map: the voyage of the *Royal Tiger* is a fantasy of British adventure among the Incas in Brazil.
2. *Great steamers, white and gold*: the ships of the Royal Mail Steam Packet Company.

How the First Letter was Written

1. *Dravidian*: ancient Indian language and name applied to the Brahmans of southern India and northern Ceylon.
2. *Hetmans*, etc.: *Hetmans*: a military title in Tsarist Russia; *Dolmans*: jackets worn by hussars; *Negus*: supreme ruler of Abyssinia; *Woons*, *Akhoonds*: Afghan titles; *Juju-men*: exponents of the cult of spirits and minor deities dwelling in objects; *Bonzes*: European name for Buddhists.
3. *Heads of Hundreds*: 'Hundred' is an English term applied to an ancient territorial division of a county, probably referring originally to a group of 100 families and later to the area occupied by them and their descendants.
4. *Platoffs*: invented word.
5. *prognathous Villeins*: *prognathous*: with projecting lower jaw; *Villeins*: medieval peasants holding tenure of land by bond service to a lord.
6. *adscript serfs*: serfs attached to the soil.
7. *heriot*: a lord provided his tenants with arms to be used in military service for him. On a tenant's death the lord reclaimed the return of the equipment.
8. *Runic magic*: runes are the oldest form of Germanic script.

How the Alphabet was Made

1. *How the Alphabet was Made*: the Western European alphabet was adapted by the Romans from the Greek alphabet and by the Greeks from the Phoenicians.
2. *Demotics*, etc.: *Demotics*: simplified popular script derived from Egyptian hieroglyphics; *Nilotics*: language used by inhabitants of the Upper Nile Valley; *Cryptics*: cryptography or cypher language; *Cufics*: early Arabic script; *Dorics*: a north-west Greek dialect from Doris; *Ionics*: in 403 B.C. the Ionian alphabet was officially adopted by Athens and supplanted the earlier competing alphabets of the various Greek states.

The Crab that Played with the Sea

1. *Perak River*: river that flows through Malaysia into the Malacca Straits.
2. *Selangor, Malacca*: formerly the British Federated Malay States, now Malaysia.
3. *Island of Bintang*: or Bintan, an island to the south of Singapore.
4. *Sarawak . . . Pahang*: a distance of 1,000 miles.
5. *P. and O.'s*, etc.: *P. and O.*: Peninsula and Oriental; *B.I.*: British India; *N.Y.K.*: Nippon, Yusen, Kaisha; *N.D.L.*: Nord Deutscher Lloyd; *M.M.*: Messageries Maritimes; *A.T.L.*: Adriatica Triestine Linea; *U.C.S.*: Union Castle Steamships; *O. and O.*: Oriental and Occidental; *D.O.A.*: Deutscher Oest Afrikan; *Shaw-Savill*: subsidiary of the White Star line: *B.S.A.*: Blue Star (an Australian line) or perhaps British and South American; *Lloyds*: London marine insurance institution (properly spelled Lloyd's).
6. *mangosteens*: a South-East Asian fruit.

The Cat that Walked by Himself

1. *fenugreek*: leguminous plant cultivated in the Mediterranean, Egypt and India.
2. *grenadillas*: the fruit of one of the tropical passion flowers.
3. *'Nenni!'*: a negative in French, meaning 'no', 'not at all'.

The Butterfly that Stamped

1. *the Lapwing who found the Water*: green plover or peewit.
2. *Hoopoe*: a beautiful southern bird.
3. *hyssop*: bushy aromatic shrub.
4. *Queen of Sabæa*: Queen of Sheba.

READ MORE IN PENGUIN

In every corner of the world, on every subject under the sun, Penguin represents quality and variety – the very best in publishing today.

For complete information about books available from Penguin – including Puffins, Penguin Classics and Arkana – and how to order them, write to us at the appropriate address below. Please note that for copyright reasons the selection of books varies from country to country.

In the United Kingdom: Please write to *Dept. EP, Penguin Books Ltd, Bath Road, Harmondsworth, West Drayton, Middlesex UB7 0DA*

In the United States: Please write to *Consumer Sales, Penguin Putnam Inc., P.O. Box 12289 Dept. B, Newark, New Jersey 07101-5289.* VISA and MasterCard holders call 1-800-788-6262 to order Penguin titles

In Canada: Please write to *Penguin Books Canada Ltd, 10 Alcorn Avenue, Suite 300, Toronto, Ontario M4V 3B2*

In Australia: Please write to *Penguin Books Australia Ltd, P.O. Box 257, Ringwood, Victoria 3134*

In New Zealand: Please write to *Penguin Books (NZ) Ltd, Private Bag 102902, North Shore Mail Centre, Auckland 10*

In India: Please write to *Penguin Books India Pvt Ltd, 11 Community Centre, Panchsheel Park, New Delhi 110017*

In the Netherlands: Please write to *Penguin Books Netherlands bv, Postbus 3507, NL-1001 AH Amsterdam*

In Germany: Please write to *Penguin Books Deutschland GmbH, Metzlerstrasse 26, 60594 Frankfurt am Main*

In Spain: Please write to *Penguin Books S. A., Bravo Murillo 19, 1° B, 28015 Madrid*

In Italy: Please write to *Penguin Italia s.r.l., Via Benedetto Croce 2, 20094 Corsico, Milano*

In France: Please write to *Penguin France, Le Carré Wilson, 62 rue Benjamin Baillaud, 31500 Toulouse*

In Japan: Please write to *Penguin Books Japan Ltd, Kaneko Building, 2-3-25 Koraku, Bunkyo-Ku, Tokyo 112*

In South Africa: Please write to *Penguin Books South Africa (Pty) Ltd, Private Bag X14, Parkview, 2122 Johannesburg*

READ MORE IN PENGUIN

RUDYARD KIPLING

'The most complete man of genius I have ever known' Henry James

'For my own part I worshipped Kipling at thirteen, loathed him at seventeen, enjoyed him at twenty, despised him at twenty-five, and now again rather admire him. The one thing that was never possible, if one had read him at all, was to forget him' George Orwell